P9-AOC-512

Head Coach

Also by Lia Riley

Hellions Angels series
Mister Hockey

Coming Soon
Virgin Territory

Brightwater series
Last First Kiss
Right Wrong Guy
Best Worst Mistake

Head Coach

A HELLIONS ANGELS NOVEL

LIA RILEY

AVONIMPULSE
An Imprint of HarperCollinsPublishers

This is a work of fiction. Names, characters, places, and incidents are products of the author's imagination or are used fictitiously and are not to be construed as real. Any resemblance to actual events, locales, organizations, or persons, living or dead, is entirely coincidental.

Excerpt from *Mister Hockey* copyright © 2017 by Lia Riley.

HEAD COACH. Copyright © 2017 by Lia Riley. All rights reserved. Printed in the United States of America. No part of this book may be used or reproduced in any manner whatsoever without written permission except in the case of brief quotations embodied in critical articles and reviews. For information, address HarperCollins Publishers, 195 Broadway, New York, NY 10007.

Digital Edition NOVEMBER 2017 ISBN: 978-0-06-266248-4
Print Edition ISBN: 978-0-06-266249-1

Cover art by Cover design by Nadine Badalaty
Cover photograph © PeopleImages / Getty Images

Avon Impulse and the Avon Impulse logo are registered trademarks of HarperCollins Publishers in the United States of America.
Avon and HarperCollins are registered trademarks of HarperCollins Publishers in the United States of America and other countries.

FIRST EDITION

17 18 19 20 21   HDC   10 9 8 7 6 5 4 3 2 1

If you purchased this book without a cover, you should be aware that this book is stolen property. It was reported as "unsold and destroyed" to the publisher, and neither the author nor the publisher has received any payment for this "stripped book."

To Chanel, Jen and A.J. . . . thank you for being a friend.
Your hearts are true. You're all pals and confidants.

P.S.: Who wants to bet Jen doesn't get this reference?

Acknowledgments

THANKS TO THE wonderfully perceptive Elle Keck who whips every book into its best version of itself, and to Emily Sylvan Kim, who isn't just an agent, but also the wind beneath my wings. Shout outs to my writing sisterhood: Jennifer Ryan (thank you for the blurb too!), Jules Barnard, A.J Pine, Chanel Cleeton (extra penguin props), Jennifer Blackwood, Megan Erickson and Natalie Blitt—you guys may all live far (too far) away, but every day it feels as if you are RIGHT THERE IN MY LIVING ROOM. To my family: Nick and the PB and J, much like Bryan Adams, I do everything for you—so much love.

Head Coach

Chapter One

STUCK IN A RUT?

THE BILLBOARD'S TACKY font splashed across the image of a blonde woman dressed in a corset, high-waist underpants and garter belt. Neve Angel scowled through her windshield at the rest of the tagline.

SHIMMY INTO A WHOLE NEW YOU!
BEGINNER BURLESQUE CLASSES AT
THE TWIRLING TASSELS

"Humph." Neve tucked an escaped strand of hair back into her bun. Ms. Blondie could pop an egg in her perfect pout and suck it. Since quitting figure skating at the age of eighteen, she had developed an allergy to glitz and glamor, favoring low-key personal grooming.

Fake lashes were out.

Foundation contouring? Negative.

Waxing? Please. She wasn't a masochist.

These days the word *pragmatic* carried far more value for her than *pretty*, thanks very much. Flicking on the radio, she relaxed her shoulders as a familiar guitar riff filled her '78 wood-paneled Jeep Wagoneer. She had an unabashed love for classic cars and classic rock, and Tom Cochrane was a guy who knew his stuff. Life *was* a highway, except forget the part about driving it "all night long."

Or driving anywhere for that matter. Satan would ice-skate through hell before this insane gridlock budged.

A silver Prius inched forward until it practically dry-humped her bumper.

Meep! The driver leaned on a wimpy-sounding horn.

Honking under these conditions was a ballsy move, akin to sitting in the last row of an airplane and standing when the cabin crew disarmed the doors—a good way to tempt ordinary citizens to commit murder.

The driver beeped again.

"Use your eyes. There's nowhere for me to go!" Neve glanced to the rearview mirror and gazed at the distinctive red cursive on the Prius's license plate.

A California driver. *Surprise, surprise.* She'd bet the loose change in the bottom of her purse that this chick was a Bay Area transplant, relocating her traffic problems to Denver along with skyrocketing home prices. The whole West was getting Californicated, from Nevada to Montana, Texas to Colorado.

The horn beeped a third time. She fisted her insulated travel mug and then took a careful sip. Madam Prius better thank her astrological chart that Neve had hot coffee within arm's reach because otherwise things could get ugly.

A minute passed.

Two.

Blessed silence reigned.

After blowing up her bangs, she pulled an everything bagel from the flimsy paper bag on the dashboard, cramming it into her mouth. In a parallel universe, Alter-Neve woke with ample time to prepare a nutritious breakfast, perhaps an acai bowl topped by sliced bananas and kiwi fruit or Greek yogurt and granola, Instagram-worthy concoctions bursting with enough omegas and fiber to make any Prius driver water their home herb garden with organic tears.

But in this world, Einstein Bros. and a dark roast had to do the job.

She brushed stray poppy seeds and flecks of dried garlic off her charcoal pants with a muffled sigh. Charcoal, i.e., dark grey . . . *not* black. Her somber closet palette might be as cheerful as a funeral home, but it never required expending mental energy at seven a.m. trying to coordinate funky colors or mix and match patterns.

From her roadside perch, the burlesque model appeared amused, as if she knew Neve ate the same hum-drum breakfast day in, day out and dressed in the same humdrum wardrobe. Or that while she might have an impressive LinkedIn profile, that didn't translate to a social life worth posting over.

Neve poked out her tongue at the model's image. This low-maintenance duckling had grown up to be . . . if not a preening swan, a confident duck.

She had a good—scratch that, great—career as a sports columnist for the *Denver Age* covering the hockey beat, and her life was too consumed by dead-lines to bother with extra fuss. Work was the priority, and as for her biological clock . . . well, it could keep right on ticking. She had another baby to grow, her side hustle, a podcast—*Sports Heaven*—that kept climbing iTunes rankings; she had even been featured in their New and Noteworthy section last month.

Rut-shmut. By any measure, Neve was doing great in her career and living her best life. Except her smirk faded as she glanced to the console clock. She'd risk missing the puck drop if traffic didn't improve soon.

Hopefully, the Hellions would get a much-needed win tonight. After their recent back-to-back champion-ships, it appeared the team's days in the sun had fallen into one serious shadow. The roster had been shaken ever since the unexpected retirement of captain Jed West last summer. This season had started as a big dis-appointment for Denver fans, and worse, whispers of NHL labor disputes were gaining traction. For the past few weeks, trusted sources had even uttered the dreaded term *lockout*—a word that kept her up at night restless and fretting.

Fingers—and toes—crossed that the powers that be would navigate through the negotiations and get the league back on track. During the 04–05 lockout, the whole season was cancelled—the worst possible outcome. Stadiums sat empty. Fans grumbled. Refs and arena workers forwent paychecks.

She shuddered, mentally elbowing away the terrible idea. Hopefully this time around, cooler heads would prevail.

And as for the Hellions, there was another place where cooler heads needed to prevail. Maybe if their goalie would practice a little Zen meditation and quit getting players sent to the penalty box every damn ga—

Meep! Meeeeeeeeep! Madam Prius hit the horn as if she'd face-planted on the steering wheel and died.

Tension migrated from Neve's neck, making the slow climb to her temples. The first throbs of a headache emerged. Between lockout worries and this racket, she might spontaneously combust. To release steam, she rolled down the window and flipped the Prius the bird before grabbing her phone off the passenger seat.

Ignoring the new—and so far unlistened-to—mindfulness podcast her friend Margot had recommended, she clicked on Byways, the popular navigation app that relied on community-sourced traffic updates to create the fastest routes. It needed to get her moving before she found herself arrested for disorderly conduct.

She plugged in the Hellions stadium address and an avatar of a pitchfork blinked from a quarter mile ahead. Her tummy performed a flawless triple-axel jump.

Rovhal30.

She took a deep breath and issued herself a stern reminder. There had never been any official confirmation that Rovhal30 was even male, but in her mind, he was six feet of strapping sexiness, lounging behind the wheel of a black Subaru Outback—a ginger-haired Ewan McGregor doppelgänger. Not *Trainspotting* Ewan either. Not even *Moulin Rouge!* Ewan. No . . . straight-up Obi-Wan Kenobi *Attack of the Clones* Ewan, with the shaggy hair and delicious beard.

One thing was for certain, the pitchfork avatar meant that Rovhal30 was a Hellions hockey fan.

Or a devil worshiper who lives in his mom's basement hand-feeding his pet bull pythons.

The pitchfork didn't budge. Rovhal30 was stuck in this traffic too. She sucked in her lower lip, debating: To message or not to message? That was the question.

No point glancing to Burlesque Blondie for advice. The model would just shimmy her tassels in a "you go, guuuurl" affirmation.

Eenie, meanie, miny . . . *ugh*. Fine. She was doing this.

NeverL8: Fancy seeing you here

She hit Send before she could second-guess her actions. Here was hoping that her tone came across more cheerful than creepy.

Rovhal30: (typing)

It always took Rovhal30 time to type back, credible evidence that he was a sixty-plus grandmother learning to operate her first smartphone, but why ruin the fantasy?

Neve drummed her thumbs on the steering wheel. She didn't bother with online dating. The idea of some random dude swiping left on her profile while taking his morning dump left a lot to be desired. But this meant that her one meaningful online relationship was with a fellow commuter on a traffic app—someone who *felt* male and *might* be attractive.

The ugly truth was that she hadn't gotten laid since the first Obama administration, even though her "office" was a locker room populated by sweaty men who rivaled Olympic gods. Every time someone heard about her job as a sports reporter, they'd gush, "Oh my God! Do you ever get to interview the players in their towels? Is it amazing?"

For the record, she had at one time or another glimpsed most of the Hellions team sans towels. As for the endless question "Is it amazing?" try asking the Louvre gallery attendant who guarded the *Mona Lisa* if they ever got used to the portrait's iconic smile.

Sure, the players were sexy with their cut bods and muscular buns, but a glimpse of wang didn't exactly send her heart racing. She was there in a professional capacity, not to be a pervert.

Rovhal30: Hello there

The Byways app made it impossible to text another driver unless the car was at a complete stop. Sadly, she too often found herself in this situation at the same time of day. A month ago, Rovhal30 had posted a community traffic update about a brush fire in the median. She'd asked a clarifying question and they'd struck up an odd friendship ever since.

Rovhal30: I've been saving a joke for you

Neve ordered the flutter in her stomach to stand down. "He probably looks like a cross between Homer Simpson and Steve Buscemi," she muttered.

But still, he'd saved a joke for her . . . which meant he thought of her. At least a little.

NeverL8: Lay it on me

Perfectly casual response—*Excellent*. For all Rovhal30 knew, she was a Byways floozy, texting with dozens of users on a regular basis.

Rovhal30: What kind of computer sings?
NevrL8: I give up
Rovhal30: A Dell

She snickered. Good one.

NeverL8: Actual LOLZ
Rovhal30: LOLZ?
NeverL8: Uh . . . like laugh out loud?
Rovhal30: Why the Z?
NeverL8: It's nonstandard spelling of the suffix "s" . . . i.e. just for fun.
Rovhal30: Remind me what i.e means again?
NeverL8: Latin for "id est"' which translates roughly to "in other words." I like it. Use it all the time.

She attached the nerdy-face emoticon for good measure and hit Send.

Pause. No response.

She chewed the inside of her cheek and waited. Still nothing.

Gah. Had she driven him away with an obscure-grammar geek out? She rocked her head back against the seat and groaned—she sucked at this. Her gaze connected with Burlesque Blondie. Fine, not only was she stuck in a rut, she won all the awards for awkward internet flirting.

It could be time to accept her spinster status, drive to

the shelter and finally choose a kitten for that cat tower that she'd bought last summer at a garage sale.

Traffic crawled forward, Rovhal30's pitchfork avatar ticked away on the upcoming off-ramp, her own exit. She gave a slow exhale and clicked out of the app.

A journalist's first obligation was to tell the truth. Hers was that she was undersexed and overworked. She wasn't living her best life. She didn't even *have* a life, too busy to even be a crazy cat lady. Her rut had masqueraded as a comfortable routine for too long. It was high time to climb out and put herself into the world. Find her inner sex kitten and make it purr.

Faster than the speed of second guesses, she snapped a photo of the phone number for The Twirling Tassels, shifted out of first gear and hit the gas.

Chapter Two

THEY WERE GOING to lose.

Tor Gunnar grabbed the Tic Tac container from his pocket, thumbed open the flip lid and popped a mint into his mouth. The five-two scoreboard told a dismal tale, one that had become increasingly familiar since the start of the season. The San Francisco Renegades, the long-standing archrivals to the Denver Hellions, were wiping the ice with them.

No heroic comeback was in the cards for tonight. Not with the way his team was disintegrating out there. Already fans were leaving their seats to get a jump start on traffic.

Third period. Five minutes left. The mint turned to dust between his molars.

The Renegades might have plunged the proverbial knife into the heart of the Hellions morale, but now they twisted the blade, antagonizing his guys, looking for ways to draw blood—both metaphorical and actual—as they settled old scores. The goalie, Donnelly, hulked in front of his net as the offense bore down. His goalie was territorial, an enraged bear protecting a cub from rogue wolves. Renegade winger Ryker Fury didn't even have the puck in possession yet had invaded the space, a clear taunt.

"Come on," Tor muttered. It was plain enough to see what was going down. Fury was out there looking to provoke a reaction. Donnelly's hotheaded temper was legendary. As much as Gunnar had tried to find new ways to cool his ass, if someone messed with him, the kid messed back. Every damn time.

"Don't do it. Don't take the bait." Tor crossed his arms. Donnelly had what it took to be a star. Someday he might be a legend—if he could learn to control his fucking temper. Even with today's score, the kid had made unbelievable saves.

Fury shouted something.

Donnelly dropped his gloves in response.

Tor hid his inner wince behind a stoic mask.

Someday Donnelly might be a superstar goalie, but today sure as shit wasn't that day.

Ryker was big—strong and mean—but Donnelly had the devil in him. His fists flew fast and hard. It wasn't long until Ryker was on the ice and Donnelly towered on top.

"Get him off, get him off," Tor roared at the team.

But it was too late. Ref made the call.

Match penalty.

Now he was down a player. Andrew Kelly, the Renegade coach, signaled who he wanted out. The Hellions star forward, Petrov, skated toward the penalty box, head down, shoulders slumped. Donnelly trailed after.

"Nate," Tor snapped. The second-string goalie was going in.

"On it, Coach." Nathan Reed checked his laces and headed out.

Donnelly didn't even glance in Reed's direction as he passed; his cheeks were flushed over his ginger beard and he breathed hard.

"Happy?" Tor growled.

"You didn't hear what that bastard said." Donnelly ripped off his mask and hurled it at the plexiglass. "Fury talked a bunch of—"

"I don't give a rat's hairless pink ass if he insulted your mama, your little sister, or your mama *and* your sister. Your job is to keep your head. Did that happen tonight?"

Donnelly stared at the floor with a sullen expression.

"I just asked you a question." Tor dropped his voice to a subzero whisper. "If you have the slightest sense of self-preservation, you're going to give me an answer."

A muscle twitched beneath Donnelly's left eye. "Lost my head."

"You're making it a habit."

"Look." He covered his face with his hand. "I'm trying not to, Coach. I'm—"

"Sucking air in my vicinity," Tor snapped. "Just get outta here and let me watch us lose in peace."

Donnelly hesitated. "I am sorry, Coach."

"So am I. I don't know what it's going to take to get through to you." Tor turned his attention back to the play. And as soon as the game was over, he got called to the owner's box to receive even worse news.

Now here he was, thirty minutes later, glaring at the Hellions locker room door while straightening his tie. Everyone on the other side would have questions, and he couldn't provide a single answer. The league negotiations had crapped out. A lockout was now in effect over salary caps, the cherry to the night's shit sundae.

Swallowing back a frustrated sigh, Tor banged open the locker room door and strode inside. All conversation muted as he marched to the center of the room and stopped short of the pitchfork emblazoned on the floor. No need to invite further bad luck by standing on top of the team logo. He drew his gaze up to his favorite Gretzky quote stenciled along the curved wall before taking in the expectant men on the benches.

These players were a unique breed. Many had left home at a young age to chase a seemingly impossible dream. Some had travelled overseas to build resumes. Most, at some point, had lived far from parents, friends and the comforts of home, forging new friendships with those who had made similar sacrifices.

It was these bonds, a brotherhood strengthened through sacrifice and physical and mental hardship, that sustained a player through tough times both on and off the ice. One of the reasons he'd insisted on the new locker room being shaped as an oval and not a square was so everyone could always see each other, no one relegated to a corner. And his commitment to keeping the focus on team over individuals had worked, at least until this season.

He pressed two fingers to his temple. He'd kill for another Jed West on the team, a natural leader with the rare combination of poise and skill.

The press corps stuffed into the room's perimeter, holding their collective breath.

Waiting.

Waiting.

The silent question was almost audible. *Will Tor Gunnar go rogue?*

The powers that be had made one thing crystal clear. With the lockout in effect, NHL staff were instructed to cut off contact with players. Violating the terms was to risk bringing down hell, everything from fines to forfeiture of future draft picks. Simply walking in here took steel balls, especially with the jackals from the press prowling the room's perimeter.

But these guys were family. *His* family. And he'd be damned if he let them go without some sort of send-off. He wanted them to know he was here. That he cared no matter what . . . win or lose, rain or shine, good times and bad. This game was bigger than a paycheck, bigger than a contract.

They were brothers in arms.

Take Munro and Nicholson on the right, defensemen with matching navy blue Mohawks. Once fierce rivals, they had even gotten into a fistfight their first year, but were now next-door neighbors in Cherry Creek. There was Petrov, the center who'd finished the game stuck in the penalty box, engaged to wingman Ericksen's twin sister.

Tor turned to face Patrick "Patch" Donnelly, hunched in front of an end locker. Even though the kid would be the death of him, he lived and breathed the sport as if it was more than a game, something vital to his existence. Patch glowered back, elbows propped on his knees, hands clasped, a picture of forced calm, his eyes as bright and menacing as a caged tiger's.

He'd demonstrated that same feral intensity at Boston College when Tor had personally recruited him after hearing rumors of a prodigy player who'd almost joined the seminary to become a priest. A walking contradiction who had a broken nose and reputation for brawling, and yet had majored in theology and was conversant in Catholic conciliar traditions—everything from Nicaea to Vatican II.

One of the journalists coughed in his fist and Tor refocused, remembering his greater audience. He'd deal with Donnelly's anger issues later. He'd come in here to exploit an elephant-sized loophole. As head coach, he might not be allowed to talk, but not all communication was verbal. Who knew what his team would get up to during the ongoing negotiations? Some might head overseas for pickup work. Others might turn to liquor and ladies. All of them better double down at the gym, remain in peak fitness, ready to hit the ice at first word.

He shot his goalie one final glance. Here was to hoping that Patch didn't retreat to a monastery on an island in the middle of the North Atlantic. He seemed the type to pull a Luke Skywalker and vanish into thin air.

Tor raked a hand through his hair and turned away with a terse nod. He'd made his point without crossing a line. Sure, the suits would be pissed, but as the door slammed, he allowed a grimly satisfied smile.

They better believe that he'd go into this lockout on his own terms.

The press poured out, hot on his heels. And—no surprise—there *she* was, front and center, jaw jutting as their gazes locked, tenacious as a goddamn bulldog even though she was as tiny as a Chihuahua.

Neve Angel.

No other reporter in this city got under his skin the same way. As much as he wanted to ignore the electric jolt that shocked him every time she was close, he had to admit he was a sucker for the pain.

He'd be tempted to find her snarky columns amusing if she wasn't so hell-bent on making him the butt of every goddamn joke. How he was too serious in his mannerisms. No nitpick was too small or too petty. She even took him to task over his fucking tie collection, and started a now-popular meme about the fact that he never changed his stoic facial expressions, no matter if the Hellions lost a game or won the championships.

Their fractious relationship made for popular YouTube fodder. She'd slip in a sly question at postgame press conferences, seemingly innocent but designed to slip under his collar and rankle. He never got the sense she was intimidated by his frosty temperament.

He could make a six-foot defenseman weep without raising his voice, but this hellcat? She'd just cock one of those defiant brows and smirk.

While not delicately pretty, she possessed an elusive allure, like starlight on water, a sort of face that a man could lose hours studying and still never grasp all its secrets.

"Care to comment on the lockout, Coach?" Todd from the AP called.

Jesus, pull it together. Tor refocused and took off walking. "This is between the players and people way above my pay grade."

"What does this mean for your losing streak?"

"How are you going to handle the Donnelly situation?"

"What are your plans to ride this out?"

"Do you think the contracts are unfair?"

But he meant it. He wasn't saying shit.

They began dropping off. Only one person kept pace.

"Coach Gunnar." Neve's voice was as brisk as her trot. "Coach Gunnar!"

"Not today, Angel. I'm not in the mood." He wasn't

going to let her track him like a damn deer all the way out to his car. And she wasn't going to back off. Time to execute plan B.

"Coach!"

"Let me be clear." He paused in front of the men's room. "It's been a long night. I gotta drain the tank, so unless you're volunteering to hold it for me, we'll have to leave things here."

He veered into the john without a backward look. Because if he did, he'd be forced to reckon with those unnerving eyes, the ones that always saw too much.

At least Neve Angel hadn't sniffed out the day's other breaking story . . .

JOIN MADDY KLINE AND DANIEL COX
AS THEY EMBARK ON A SHARED LIFE . . .

The invite had arrived in the mail this morning. Maddy had mailed the damn invitation to his office, probably a silent reminder to the day she'd walked out, saying "It's your job or me. Choose."

And he did.

Maddy had moved on and it was all water under the bridge by this point. But her upcoming marriage shone a spotlight on the fact that he was still stuck. Work was his whole identity. He didn't know who he was if he wasn't "Coach."

But with this lockout in effect, he might be forced to find out.

Chapter Three

"I'll hold it for him all right," Neve snarled at her fellow reporters. "And then I'll tie that man's dick into a bow."

And if his insinuation about her hand being anywhere in the vicinity of his Big Lebowski left her mouth dry, it was just a reminder that she needed to drink more water.

Hydration was important.

"What do we do? Draw straws for who goes in after him?" Bill from ESPN reached into his pocket as if to pull out a handful.

Everyone wore identical, terrified "not I" expressions. Tor Gunnar was a force of nature and no one had enough bravery—or stupidity—to bug him during a piss. They could find a urinal cake shoved down their throat for their trouble.

Neve noted the group mired in indecision and turned for the exit with a one-shouldered shrug. While they all clucked like nervous hens, she'd swoop in like a hawk and snatch the scoop.

"Didn't expect *you* to give up so fast, Angel," someone shouted.

She didn't reply, hoping they'd laugh off her finger bomb. Because maybe . . . just maybe . . . her hunch on the coach was right on the money. There was the old adage "Keep your friends close and enemies closer." It totally applied when it came to her hate-tionship with Tor Gunnar.

She didn't break into a run until she had pushed out the exit into the crisp night air. The door snicked shut and she dug in, arms pumping, messenger bag knocking against her hip.

Thank God she'd been setting the treadmill to eight-minute miles at the gym.

She skidded around the corner and straight into a good news/bad news moment.

The good news was that her instincts were right. Tor Gunnar wasn't the type to be treed like a cougar by a pack of bloodhounds. He was far too wily. The men's bathroom window screen lay on the pavement, right where he'd kicked it out with one of those big lace-up leather boots he wore, the ones that went well with that tailored suit that matched his dark blue eyes. In the streetlight, they shone a rich twilight blue, a color that made smart girls stupid.

The bad news was that she gaped at him from an uncomfortably close vantage point. They stood chest to chest, or boobs to ribs to be exact. She'd smacked right into him, but it wasn't like running into a wall. No. There was nothing wall-like going on here. This was all man, flesh and blood, even if he was as immovable as mortared brick.

"Well, well, well." She forced her body to lock up, stiffening her muscles so as not to betray the slightest tremble, even as a hot wind blew through her ladyparts, clearing away the dust and cobwebs. "Fancy meeting you here. That was some game tonight. You getting your goalie enrolled in an anger-management class or what?"

Muscles bunched in Tor Gunnar's jaw, ones that never seemed to appear unless she was around. The rest of the press pool called it his "Angel anger muscles." She wasn't one to toot her own horn, but when it came to pissing off this man, she possessed a remarkable gift.

"You never quit, do you?" His tone was flat, but he didn't protest or ask what she was doing there. He gave her that credit. As much as he rubbed her the wrong way, she respected him as a worthy adversary.

"I aim to live my life so that my tombstone can say *Nevertheless, she persisted*."

That earned a snort. She'd take that as her in.

"Anyway, look on the bright side. The lockout news was even worse than the final score, am I right?"

He didn't take the bait. Nor did she expect him to. He was far too disciplined to drop a useful quote so easily, at least not right away. She'd have to play him like a conductor, work him up until he sang like a pissed-off canary.

"My source in the commissioner's office says that there's a chance this could drag on for the rest of the season. But then maybe it's a blessing."

Those twilight eyes darkened to midnight black. Most people would shrink at the warning.

Good thing that she wasn't most people.

"A blessing?" He leaned in, his voice a lethal whisper.

Something shifted in the air between them, a magnetic force that sucked air from her lungs.

Her shrug was a study in nonchalance even as a shiver shuddered down her spine. "It would be such a shame for the Hellions to have an epic flop after enjoying back to back years on top. But there's no way your team is even going to qualify for the playoffs. Lends credence to the idea that the real credit for the Hellions success was Jed West."

"Bullshit." His carved features were schooled in careful impassivity. "My team's still finding their feet with the new lineup. If the knuckleheads on the Board of Governors pulled their heads out of their deskbound asses for two seconds, they'd see . . ." He froze, realizing what he had done. Two lines etched his high forehead. Two more between his arrogant brows. Cracks in the stony veneer.

"Mmm-hmm. Knuckleheads . . . and deskbound asses—now, there's a turn of phrase." Neve licked her lips in slow triumph. "I'm afraid their rebuttal won't be nearly as flowery."

Shadows haunted his high cheekbones, the angles sharp and unforgiving, inherited from whatever Viking ancestor also bestowed that thick blond hair. It didn't take much imagination to picture Tor Gunnar's doppelgänger plundering hapless Scandinavian villages during the Dark Ages. He looked warlike even when standing still and breathing.

And yet . . .

And yet.

She didn't step back in retreat. He couldn't take a full step forward either, not when she was still squished against him. The only feature not absolutely brutal in his face was his wide mouth, the bold, sensual lips that hovered close to hers as he bent and whispered in a rasp, "What the fuck do you want?" His breath held a trace of wintergreen.

She was ready to dish back a serving of sass, except no plucky banter came out. Only a moan, one that hitched raggedly on the end note and carried a heavy dose of breathlessness.

Her brain stuttered, unable to get back in gear. What was she doing, standing here dazed and confused, thinking less about getting a scoop and more on what it would be like if *he* scooped *her* up? Hauled her against the brick wall behind them. Tore open her shirt and sucked her nipples through the thin cotton of her bra with those big mean lips?

His gaze lasered on hers in stunned surprise, as if

he'd been granted security clearance to review her most confidential fantasies. A hum buzzed through her stomach. No gentle fluttering of butterflies, but a hive of bees, and it wasn't clear if they were about to sting or make sweet, sweet honey.

Somewhere a door slammed and voices filled the night. The press pool rounded the corner. The best and brightest had finally pieced together what she had deduced two minutes earlier.

Tor was making a getaway.

Her face heated; thank God it was night. She moved back, but her gestures were awkward, clumsy even. Restless energy coursed through her. In the distance a siren wailed.

"Shit," Tor muttered.

Her colleagues gaped, their eyes still adjusting to the darkness.

"What's going on?" Todd's nose had gone red from the biting November wind. He'd invited Neve out for drinks once. When she'd turned him down, he'd inquired if she was a lesbian, as if that was the only plausible explanation.

"Nothing." Tor strode towards his car.

"Didn't look like nothing a second ago," Todd kept pushing. "What gives? You two have a thing?"

"Yeah. Right." His laugh was dismissive. "Sorry, not into cold fish. If I got off on a dick freeze, I'd fuck a penguin." With that he shot off without so much as a backward glance.

Neve didn't flinch. Later she was going to be proud of that fact. Instead she pursed her mouth into what might appear to be mild amusement. She could nail this look better than those double salchows from her figure skating days. No, she didn't give a single sign that Coach's words sliced through her softest, most sensitive pieces.

Cold fish. Cold fish? Cold fish! Hell no, she was a red-hot barracuda of revenge.

His Porsche roared to life, mirroring the blood accelerating through her veins. She watched him tear from the parking lot with steely-eyed resolve. Freedom of speech was all well and good, but Mr. Fuck-a-Penguin had issued serious fighting words.

This meant war.

Language could be wielded like a weapon; she knew that better than anyone, and with the lockout in place, she was going to have to get more creative with her story ideas. Readers, and her pain-in-the butt editor—Scott Moore—loved top-five lists. She mentally rubbed her hands together as she selected the perfect clickbait title to pitch:

Top Five Worst Coaches in the NHL

Guess who'd just earned himself a primo spot?

Chapter Four

TOR STALKED INTO his foyer and kicked the front door closed behind him. He bypassed the couch and flat-screen in favor of the kitchen, where he opened the liquor cabinet and removed a dusty bottle of Johnnie Walker Blue Label. He didn't drink much, but when the urge struck then he didn't mess around.

The new leopard gecko that his daughter Olive had suckered him into buying sat on a log under its aquarium heat lamp. He checked its water. His ten-year-old daughter hadn't been able to decide on a suitable name before her mother had picked her up and so it was stuck nameless until her return.

"What was I supposed to say?" he asked the lizard.

The gecko stared back, eyes wide, body unmoving.

"I'm telling you, buddy, Neve Angel drives me to drink."

He picked up the bottle, ready to pour half the contents down his throat if it meant softening the hard-on busting through his pants. This bad news day was made all the worse by the fact that his traitor cock had been standing at attention ever since his parking lot encounter with Neve.

"I envy you, you know," he muttered to the gecko. "Happily alone. Minding your own business. Good life."

He poured a hefty double shot into the tumbler, no ice, and took it to his master-bedroom bathroom, shooting back the amber-colored bourbon in a single gut-searing gulp before shedding his work clothes.

No need for a tie for a while.

He ripped it off his neck and tossed it onto the stone floor. Once naked, he stepped into the shower and turned on the spray without waiting for the temperature to adjust. The chill before the hot water would douse the throb in his balls.

A quick glance at his shaft showed the thought for what it was—a whole lot of wishful thinking. He gripped himself hard at the root, hissing more from the sensation shooting to the pit of his gut than the now-hot water needling his bare chest. He eschewed lubing with the body wash perched on the ledge, stroking himself the old-fashioned way. He kept his rhythm methodical, *up and down, down and up, up and down, down and twist over the head.* His other hand braced on the granite tile.

But try as he might to make this a run-of-the-mill jack off, his mind unlocked a back door and forbidden thoughts slipped through, ones where Neve watched him, her dark eyes riveted on his cock as she devoured every inch.

His fingers on the wall curled into his palm at the idea, making a fist, and before he pounded it against the stone in a half-hearted, frustrated punch, he paused to imagine what it would be like to slide his hand down and cup the back of her head, to press her to his groin, urge her to take everything he had to give. Her wavy dark hair always looked so lush, so shiny. Yeah. He'd grab a great greedy fistful as her tight little mouth took him straight to heaven.

He rocked his hips harder. How long had it been since anyone had touched him?

Not since Maddy left.

A pathetic fact when so many puck bunnies would be willing to spend a night with a championship coach. He registered on a basic level that he was good-looking. At forty there was no sign of middle-aged paunch. He kept his body lean with a shit ton of running. But random hookups had never been his thing. Not even in his twenties. He was a feast-or-famine kind of guy, either in a serious long-term relationship or alone.

And more often than not . . . the latter.

He increased his rhythm, frowning at the sound of friction, the rasp of skin against skin. Hard for a guy to lie to himself when he was working over his dick. Neve Angel had lodged under his skin with all the ease of a barbed cactus. God, that woman was a pain in the ass.

Always quick to call out a question that he had hoped would pass unasked, and with that small pouting smile that communicated one thing: *Gotcha.*

Heat licked up his neck. He needed to come, to purge his body of the poison, the unwanted attraction toward his small, sleek nemesis. But his body revolted. Unwilling to grant him the victory of an easy release.

Instead, desire pressed like a weight to the pit of his belly, increasing in pressure bit by bit until a shudder ran through his quads, the muscles tightening and bunching in small, involuntary contractions that sent microbursts of heat up his hamstrings and a targeted blast of heat to his sac. He removed the hand propping his weight against the tile, slid it down, his rough palm caressing the thin, ruddy skin encasing his balls, and expelled a ragged "Fuck."

The spray peppered his chest in tiny licks. As beads of water trickled over his sensitive, flat nipples, the tip of his cock held a gleam that had nothing to do with the shower. He pressed the flat of his thumb down hard over his head, barking out a frustrated moan.

"Come on," he ordered himself, his cock.

All in good time, Bossy. He imagined Neve's annoyed tone with such pitch-perfect clarity that the orgasm took him by surprise.

His cock jerked in his hand, the deep, aching muscles clenching even after he came with a roar that might have made his elderly neighbors dial 911, thinking he'd just been murdered.

He leaned his forehead against the tiles, splaying both hands for balance. But his neighbors wouldn't be more wrong. Because he was more alive than he'd been in recent memory. His nerves tingled. His body was primed, ready to take on the whole damn world.

A frown tugged at his lips. As awesome as he felt, this wasn't good. What the fuck had he been thinking? This was a dangerous road. He better turn around and get his ass back to safer ground.

After flicking off the shower, he stepped out and reached for a towel, not the plushy soft one either. No, he grabbed the scratchy thin grey one that he'd had since his college days and for some reason never trashed. He scraped it over his damp body until his skin was red. He couldn't be getting his rocks off to Neve Angel. She was the enemy who baited him every chance she got. She'd even written a piece on his divorce for a lifestyle mag. Probably earned a pretty fucking penny and took a vacation on his personal misery. She was just another jackal who feasted on the remains of other people's lives.

If this was what happened when he stopped thinking about work, then he was in for a world of trouble. He tied the towel around his hips and stalked back to the kitchen, empty tumbler clutched in one fist. There was only one thing to do with this secret attraction—numb it with more whisky. Time to give himself one hell of a hangover, one that ruined him so much that he'd never be able to equate Neve Angel with sexy times again.

A WEEK LATER, and there was still no deal to end the lockout doldrums. Neve shuffled into The Twirling Tassels and eyed the line of folding chairs with a growing sense of trepidation. There was a world of difference between having a big idea and executing it.

"Yeah. So. Maybe this isn't such a good idea," she murmured to the two women a step behind: her little sister, Breezy, and their friend Margot, who looked effortlessly sexy in high-cut black dancer pants and a midriff-baring royal blue tank top that revealed toned abs still bronzed from her summer trip to Baja.

"Well, for starters you should have worn heels," Margot hissed, pointing to her own Louboutins for emphasis. "The welcome letter specified that—"

"She doesn't own heels," Breezy sighed.

In contrast to Margot's eagerness, her sister's face was tight with unease, the same way it was whenever she was called on to do something athletic. But she still rocked a pair of ruffled hot pants that showed off her every curve.

Neve's heart sank into the soles of her Converse. Breezy's beehive and cat's eye makeup gave her a smoky Adele appearance, while Margot looked like the classic girl next door, albeit one who'd shimmy down the apple tree outside her bedroom window to get jiggy in the neighborhood park. But in her grey yoga pants and UC Boulder college T-shirt, Neve felt about as sexy as a mushroom.

This was a big mistake. Huge. She was a confident duck, not a sexy swan, and leaving her rut didn't mean climbing Striptease Mountain. Her jaw clenched. There was one person to blame for this serious overreach.

Tor Gunnar with his cold-fish, penguin-fucking comments.

As if on cue, bump-and-grind jazz music began to play and the other students took their positions straddling the chairs.

She adjusted her bun, stomach queasy. If the Hellions coach hadn't acted like the idea of being attracted to her was a joke, she'd have never pulled up the burlesque studio's number that she'd photographed while stuck in traffic. And she'd have never been irritated enough to go out for emergency drinks with Margot and Breezy at their favorite bar.

And she certainly wouldn't have knocked back three Jack and Diet Cokes before revealing Tor's smart-ass comments.

After Margot and Breezy had wrapped up their gasps and "Oh, honey, no! What is he talking about? What a jerk!" comments, she'd sheepishly confessed her half-baked burlesque idea with every expectation that they'd laugh her under the table.

Instead, Margot had slammed her hand down on the table so hard that one of the empty glasses went flying halfway toward the pool tables. "Yes," she shouted. "Yes! Yes! Yes!" She banged her hand as if in the throes of pleasure. "You need to do this. Take back the power, hold up your head and be the badass woman not afraid to shake her booty. Heck, all of us should get more bow-chicka-wow-wow. It's good for the soul."

"Speak for yourselves," Breezy had sniffed, even while her eyes danced. "If I have any more bow-chicka then I'm not going to be able to sit down for a week."

"No one likes a humble bragger," Margot had scolded with mock severity. "Although you can't keep secrets about Jed West's bedroom prowess all to yourself. Throw us a bone . . . er." She'd waggled her eyebrows. "Like does he talk dirty? Huh? Huh?"

"I'm not telling you that!" Breezy looked as if she'd stuck her face in a plate of ketchup. "It's private." She'd fallen hard for Jed West, captain of the Hellions Angels over the summer after he'd showed up for a literacy event at her library. One thing led to another and the rest of history. After concerns due to symptoms arising from a nasty concussion, he retired from the sport and took a position coaching college hockey for Denver University. Breezy had moved into his condo and cue the cheesy happy-ever-after music.

In her desire to save Breezy from more embarrassment, Neve had declared they would sign up right there. Now she wished she'd demanded her sister give Margot the gossip.

"Bonjour, bonjour." A svelte fortysomething woman bustled into the room in a black bodysuit and fishnets. "I am Madam Monique and you are 'ere for ze beginner 'eel class, *non*?" She had a French accent to boot. Striking a pose, hands on her hips, she surveyed the class.

There were ten women in total, all dressed in fashionable dance wear and ready to flaunt their moneymakers. Neve caught her own dumpy reflection in the studio mirror. She looked as if she'd gotten lost on the way to FBI boot camp training.

"*Alors*, where are your 'eels?" Madam Monique cast a finger to Neve like a Renaissance painting of an Old Testament god.

"Uh . . . I don't have any," Neve mumbled.

Someone in the back row tittered.

Her cheeks went from warm to scalding. It was like being back in middle school again.

"But zis is a 'eel class." Madam Monique seemed honestly confused.

That made two of them. Her mouth dried. Why had she signed up again? In trying to mentally one-up Tor Gunnar, she was only serving to humiliate herself.

"That's what I told her," Margot sang out.

"Stop being the teacher's pet." Breezy giggled.

"Next class, 'ave the 'eels and an outfit that makes you feel fabulous, okay?" Madam Monique refocused on the rest of the class. "Zee dances you master in zis class will change your life. You will 'ave power. Sex appeal. Radiate charm and confidence. Men will see you coming and ooooh . . . notice you going."

One girl raised her hand. "When do we get to wear the pasties?"

"What's a pastie?" Breezy murmured.

"No clue," Neve shot back. "But I think it's making me hungry."

That set Margot to giggling, and the problem with Margot's giggle was that it was contagious, a hiccupping snort that made the listener helpless against joining in.

Neve wheezed and Madam Monique froze. "Ah. *Bien.* Our first volunteer," she purred, crooking her finger to beckon Neve forward. Her grin was like a cat who'd eaten the cream. "*Mais oui,* a most excellent idea."

Neve drew forward with as much enthusiasm as a prisoner approaching the guillotine.

"Remove your shirt."

"Come again?" Neve asked. All she had on was a sports bra, one that used to be white until it got mixed up with Breezy's red sweater in the wash a few years ago when they were roommates. Now, not only was it old and stretched out, it was also the same hue as a slice of baloney.

"*Oui.* Your shirt," Madam Monique declared imperiously. "Strip."

An hour later Neve hurtled into the studio parking lot.

"To The Watering Hole, stat," she muttered to Breezy and Margot when they emerged a moment later.

"You were a good sport . . . trying on those pasties for the class demonstration," Breezy said. "But yes, after that drinks are in order. I'm going to message Jed and let him know our plans. He wanted to meet up and hear all the class."

Neve groaned. Madame Monique had made her try on the nipple adhesive coverings and do a shimmy in front of everyone.

"Did you mean to get your arm stuck in the bra strap like that?" Margot asked, a little too innocently.

"That's it, not only are you buying the first round, you're also the designated driver," Neve growled, shoving her Jeep Wagoneer keys at Margot. "Ugh, that was an hour of my life that I can never get back." She crawled into the Wagoneer's backseat, letting Breezy and Margot take the front. "I think my tassels are twirled out."

"No way. It was your bright idea to sign us up for the whole month," Breezy said sternly. "I coughed up the money and it's nonrefundable."

"*Blech.* Isn't Jed your sugar daddy? Come on. You can't be hurting for cash," Neve snapped, giving herself over to her black mood.

"Neve Frances Angel." Breezy whirled. "I'm giving you a pass for that comment. But it's the only one. Jed is my *boyfriend.* He isn't Mister Hockey or a punch line to your jokes."

"Okay, okay. I'm sorry," Neve muttered even as envy flared, a toxic brand of jealousy that she hated harboring anywhere in the vicinity of Breezy. Anyone could see that her sister was gaga for Jed, and not only that, the feeling was mutual. When she walked into a room, it was like she was the only person who existed for him.

No one had ever looked at Neve in that way. And before Jed, no one had ever looked at Breezy like that either, not even her old fiancé. But now she'd won the relationship golden ticket and was skipping off like she had an all-access pass to Willy Wonka's Chocolate Factory while Neve stayed stuck behind the gate.

"How do I get to The Watering Hole from this side of the city?" Margot asked. She had been raised in Portland and had come to Denver to attend yoga teacher training a few years ago. She still got turned around on city streets.

"I think I know but let me double check Byways in case it can get us there faster." Neve pulled up the route, and let the monotone voice call out the directions.

She idly watched the app screen as Margot drove through the city streets. Better than remembering Madame Monique's disapproving "tut-tut" as she ordered Neve to loosen up and "try and 'ave fun."

Neve's heart paid a surprise visit to her throat. Then there it was . . . the red-pitchfork avatar appeared on the screen.

Rovhal30 was out on the town tonight, and if the GPS signal was anything to be believed, he was currently in the parking lot at The Watering Hole.

Holy crap.

And here it was, ladies and gentlemen, the moment of truth. Her fantasy was about to become—for better or worse—a reality.

Chapter Five

"WHAT THE HELL happened?" Tor barked into his phone in lieu of a greeting, pacing the back corner of the bar parking lot. The text message had come in as he was walking inside.

> Inger: I had a fall at the climbing gym. In the hospital. Okay. Mostly.

Typical Inger. To describe his sister as understated was an understatement in and of itself. She was like the Black Knight in *Monty Python and the Holy Grail*, could be limbless and still chirping about how it was merely a flesh wound.

"X-rays came back twenty minutes ago. They're telling me that my femur suffered a hairline fracture." She blew out a frustrated breath. "And my kneecap is pretty much shattered. There were some other things, but I forget. Doc thinks I can kiss my spring climbing trip to Yosemite goodbye. I'd be mad, but I'm hopped up on so much Vicodin that I don't even know my own name. Who are you again?"

He didn't smile. Nothing about the situation was remotely funny. "Do you need me to get on a plane?" Inger lived in Minneapolis with her boyfriend and two corgis. They saw each other infrequently, but stayed in touch via short weekly calls.

"Nah, I'll live. At my age though, I should use a harness. That's a weird word, right, *harness*?" Her normally crisp voice slurred. *"Climbing harnessssss."*

"Inger. Focus," he snapped. "I'm serious." His sister wasn't a rambler. She was a corporate attorney with a reputation for precision speech. She must be pretty messed up. "I can come, just say the word. Is Jason looking after you? Making sure you are getting pain meds? Staying hydrated?"

"So protective, little brother." There was a smile in her voice, but the tightness underneath made it clear that she was in a lot of pain. "He's being a big help. But this means I have to bail on being your plus one to Maddy's wedding. I'm getting transferred to a rehab facility for a week or two."

"Don't give me a second thought, just focus on getting better. I'll be fine. Maddy and I are on good terms. Olive will miss you though." He hoped his tone was convincing. He didn't want to be a selfish asshole. His sister had sustained a serious injury, one that required a lengthy recuperation. He'd put in a call to a clinic he knew in the cities and get her squared away with some kick-ass PT. And she was right, her boyfriend would look after her. Jason worked from home for a tech firm and was devoted to her.

But now Tor would have to endure his ex-wife's wedding alone. It wasn't that he longed to have Maddy back. Not at all. They'd gotten married for plenty of the wrong reasons and too few of the right. But still.

The fact that she'd been the one to walk out had left a hurt that went deep. These days the pain was so familiar as to be a part of him, like the twinges in his lower back, old injuries from his days playing for the University of Minnesota.

She'd made him choose between work and love. But when it came down to it, he loved to work. He didn't just do his job, he *was* his job—and when she'd rejected that part of him, it'd felt like she'd rejected all of him. If she'd really understood him, she'd have respected that he didn't coach for glory or a paycheck . . . He did it because it was what he was meant to do. And yeah, the grueling NHL schedule demanded that sometimes he'd miss an event or a birthday, but he'd do his damndest to make it up. He'd established a FaceTime date with his daughter every night he was on the road. But his efforts were never enough. Maddy had crafted a narrative wherein she played second string to hockey and eventually he gave up and gave in to her story, becoming less emotionally involved.

Until she was gone.

He wasn't proud. But that's how it happened.

Inger called it "growing apart." He didn't know what to call it except a failure.

And he hated failing.

He bit down on the toothpick in the corner of his mouth, snapping the thin wood in two before spitting the shards onto the parking-lot asphalt. He'd given up smoking cold turkey when Olive was born. Toothpicks still took the edge off.

Two guys stumbled out of The Watering Hole front door doing a bad rap impression of Eminem's "Lose Yourself."

"What's going on over there?" Inger asked, her words slurry, sleepy.

"Don't worry about it. I'm getting a drink with Jed."

"Ooooh, *Jed West* Jed?" She perked. Woman always did when hearing that name. "How's he doing in post-Hellions life?"

"Good." Great actually. The asshole was happier than he'd ever been, coaching on the college level and in love. Tor wanted to be happy for his friend, and he was, most of the time, when he wasn't cursing him as a son of a bitch for his good luck.

He'd found a woman who loved him for who he was. No apologies.

"Wow, thanks for the newsy gossip," Inger teased. "Hey." She yawned. "I should get some sleep. Jason will be back soon and the nurses wake me up every two hours on their rounds."

"Go. I'll check back in tomorrow."

"Love you, Twinkle Toes," she said sleepily.

"You too." And he did, even if he could never bring himself to say it. When he looked for the right way to express feelings, the words formed a logjam in his throat. He knew he could be dismissed as an asshole, but that was bullshit. He just didn't wear his heart on his sleeve.

The way he'd grown up, it was far safer to hide it behind a fortress of bone and ice.

His phone buzzed. He checked his texts. Nothing. He frowned. That was weird. Then he noticed his Byways app had a message. He clicked it open and a stupid grin tugged the corner of his mouth.

> NeverL8: Hey! Not to sound like a stalker, but are you at The Watering Hole by any chance? I'm on my way and spotted your avatar. Maybe we could meet up and curse Prius drivers in person?

He lowered the phone and stared at the brick wall of the popular neighborhood bar. *Shit.* He wasn't prepared. He'd been chatting with this woman online for a month, the sassy one who used an avatar of angel wings. It didn't mean much, just idle conversation when stuck in gridlock. And yet . . .

His stomach muscles tightened. And yet it *had*

meant a lot. He'd found himself looking forward to the short encounters. He wasn't a guy who made easy small talk. He wasn't given to flirting. He knew he was too serious and should smile more.

A Jeep Wagoneer tore into the parking lot and hit the curb. Music blared from the windows, some bubblegum pop song that made his teeth hurt from all the sugary sweetness.

"Damn it," he muttered. The racket from that tin can was making it hard to calm down. He dragged a hand through his hair and released a frustrated breath.

His contact with NeverL8 was such a small part of his day, and yet it felt . . . fuck it . . . pure. A moment where he wasn't the coach. Or Daddy. Or the ex. He was just a guy in traffic who could share a joke. It had always been a talent of his, remembering punch lines. Guess it was the one good quality Dad ever gave him.

Nils Gunnar was the man of the party. The self-proclaimed King of St. Paul. He had a joke for every occasion and a booming laugh heard down the block. The problem was that the jokes ran out the minute he got back home.

It took effort to put those memories on lockdown, but Tor tried his best.

Instead he scanned the busy road, bustling with Saturday-night traffic, and waited to meet his mystery friend. What would she be driving?

"Tor? Oh my God, it *is* you!" Breezy Angel ran across the parking lot, the smile on her face bigger than her tiny black shorts. "Jed didn't mention you were here too!"

"Surprise, surprise." Tor gave a tense smile. His buddy hadn't mentioned that he was including his new live-in girlfriend in on their beer plans, but what the hell, it was impossible not to like Breezy.

"Are you coming inside with us?" she asked. "Because oh my God! We have got to tell you all about this class we just went to."

"And if you're lucky we will perform our newly learned chair routine." The leggy brunette piped up from beside her, propping a hand on her narrow waist and giving him an appreciative once-over.

"My best friend Margot," Breezy said by way of introduction. "And of course you know my little big sister . . . Neve."

And there she was, small and dark, hanging a few steps back in the shadows. If Breezy was all curves and Margot was legs for days, Neve was self-contained and sleeker than a black cat. She had the sort of direct gaze that dared others to try to pet her, but he knew if he ever attempted it she'd unsheathe her claws.

"I'm staying out here," he muttered. "Waiting to meet . . . a friend." *Of sorts.*

"Oh okay, yeah, sure." Breezy turned to Margot with a shrug and they both disappeared into the bar.

Neve loitered, studying his face. "I'm not used to seeing you out of a suit," she said after a beat. "You look different in jeans."

There were a hell of a lot of things going on inside that sentence, and he hated how much curiosity he had over every unspoken word.

"What are you doing, Angel?" he asked dryly, tapping a hand against his denim-encased thigh. "Still trying to get me on the record for the lockout?"

"Meh, resist all you want. It's just a matter of time." She fluffed her bangs and swung her gaze to some undefinable point in the distance. What was that, a smirk?

"What's so funny?" he pushed.

"Life," she answered cryptically. "Except I think the joke's on me."

"Any time you want to speak in plain sentences, I'm all ears."

"Cool. Until then, why don't you keep waiting for your big mystery date, Rovhal30?"

The name hit him like a stick to the face, snapping everything into place. He shoved a hand into his pocket to resist slapping his forehead.

The wings.

The pun on her name.

Christ, could he be more of a fucking idiot?

But as he met her glare, he realized that was exactly what he was.

"*You're* NeverL8?"

Chapter Six

Was the man really so miserly that he couldn't spare a single glance in her direction? Neve leaned back in the booth and studied Tor's profile. If she wasn't so annoyed with his determination to ignore her, she'd have deemed his tenacity rather sexy.

She wrapped her fingers around her thumb and squeezed for good measure. So sue her, she'd modified a noun with the adjective *sexy* in relation to Tor Gunnar. And God help her, she wasn't even tipsy. In fact, she hadn't been able to swallow more than half of a mouthful of her margarita ever since Margot plonked it down fifteen minutes ago. And it was top-shelf Patron Silver, for crying out loud.

Now Margot was back at the bar flirting with a dreadlocked bartender, his tight white T-shirt molded to his defined pecs, the color popping the deep bronze of his skin. Meanwhile, Jed and Breezy cuddled across the booth, cooing and whispering between kisses while studiously ignoring the curious glances from onlookers. Neve glanced at her watch. The love birds had exactly one more minute before she stepped in and made a citizen's arrest for the crime of PDA.

"Disgusting, isn't it?"

"Stop the presses." She glanced to Tor with a start. "Are you speaking mouth words to me?"

His glacial expression had the curious effect of heating her down to the tips of her toes. "As you don't have my ex-captain's tongue shoved halfway down your throat . . . then yeah. I suppose I am."

Neve raised her brows. "You know, those might be the most words you've ever voluntarily spoken to me."

He arched one of his own blond brows right back. "Hope you enjoyed the experience."

"I'm willing to be generous in my Yelp review." A small smile tugged her lips. "Let's go with a three out of five."

"Three?"

His unexpected smile drew her in. And it shouldn't. Tor was good-looking, but so were most guys in her line of work. After all, she spent her days in the company of professional athletes.

So what was it about this particular man that quickened her pulse?

But while her mind might stage a freak-out, her face never would. "What's the problem?" She kept her features a mirror to his own, one of cool, calculated amusement. "That's better than fifty percent."

He paused.

They might be enemies, but together they won at awkward pauses.

"I should have known," he said at last.

She was physically incapable of allowing this man to make a vague statement her without pushback. "Explain."

"I should have known you were NeverL8. Your name was right there, not to mention those avatar angel wings."

"Can't say you earned a Scooby snack for your sleuthing skills, Shaggy." She winked.

His surprised bark of laughter hit her belly like a shot, swirling through her veins with intoxicating force. She'd heard his laugh before of course, in the locker room over the years, always while talking to one of his guys. But never at *her*. She liked it, she realized, crossing her arms tight across her chest. A lot.

Too much.

"Excuse me. I have to pay a visit the little girls' room," she announced, almost tipping her untouched drink in her hurry to stand. Had someone turned up the heat? The room felt overwarm and too damn crowded. Breathing space. What she needed was breathing space.

Better yet, thinking space.

Pushing through the crowd, she thought Tor called out her name, but she didn't want to check only to discover that it had been wishful thinking.

She stormed ahead, chin down, arms swinging. Wishful thinking had bitten her in the butt enough in the past hour. The delicious Ewan McGregor fantasy of her Byways dreams had turned out to be a nightmare— worse, a guy who hated her guts.

A guy she hated right back, of course.

This was all a lot to take in. Too much to process.

She was a simple girl. Maybe her life had been stuck in a rut, but so what? Ruts provided protection from the elements, gave shelter—a cozy hiding place. If she stayed in a rut, she would never have to do anything uncomfortable, like put herself out there.

No bathroom line, thank God. She pushed into the single-stall unisex space, the door banging a cinder-block wall riddled by graffiti art and old concert posters. After turning the lock, she marched to the sink, flicked on the tap and splashed cold water onto her face.

One of the benefits of never wearing makeup was having no mascara to ruin. She splashed and splashed again, her nerves going off like a Fourth of July fireworks show.

"You are experiencing a normal physiological reaction," she reassured the panicked expression staring back in the mirror while registering the fact that her face wasn't the only thing wet. "It's time to take Breezy's advice and invest in a battery-operated boyfriend."

She had always felt silly when perusing sex toys online, as if she was an imposter with no business owning clitoris-fluttering rings or body-warming lube.

On the rare occasion when she'd attempted to explore the thousands of ways to get off in the world, she would always end up back at eighteen years old, hearing the words of a rival coach after she failed to qualify for the national figure-skating championships.

"Neve Angel?" She'd overheard him scoffing to one of his skaters while she curled behind a row of folding chairs, bawling her eyes out. He'd glanced in her direction with a sneer, as if sensing her presence. "With the jaw and bushy brows?" he'd said a little louder. "That skinny little bitch isn't prime-time, and the judges instinctively sensed it tonight. Trust me, she's no threat. She's nothing at all."

After they had walked away, she'd scrubbed her mouth clean of lipstick with the back of her hand. Hard.

She'd goodbye to the world of glitz and glamor, hung up her skates and never looked back. Her sister had often complimented her looks, and seemed like she meant it, but when Neve was alone with the bathroom mirror, all she could ever think was *That jaw . . . those brows . . . skinny little bitch*. Finally, Neve had avoided her reflection altogether. Instead, she put her head down and worked.

Forget flirting.

Forget fun.

She'd doubled down on being serious. And if she wasn't sexy enough to tempt men like Tor Gunnar, welp, so be it. She was used to it. It's just how she rolled.

Sometimes people mentioned her "bold brows" or "strong features" as if they were good things. And she didn't want to be a self-loathing woman nitpicking her faults. The last thing she wanted to do was admit that in a perfect world she'd love to possess the pixie face and effortless grace of Audrey Hepburn in *Funny Face*.

Because this wasn't a perfect world.

Far from it.

Smoothing her hair, she straightened, sucking in her abs and squaring her shoulders. She *would* go buy that cat. Eventually she'd figure out a way to ignore the hole in her heart, the one that ached to be filled even more than the lonely place between her legs.

And that was saying a lot.

"Enough." She dabbed the mysterious moisture collecting in the corners of her eyes.

Forget burlesque classes and trying to be sexy. She'd construct a roof on her rut and call it a home. After all, this was the twenty-first century. She could take care of her own business one self-administered orgasm at a time.

She had enough time on her hands with the stupid lockout in effect.

Sniffing twice, she turned to the door. Now that she had a plan, all she needed to do was survive this stupid night and that stupidly sexy man, who had managed to ruin the one bit of stupid harmless flirtation she had in her life. *Bye, bye, Byways.*

Good thing she'd turned in her "Top Five Worst Coaches in the NHL" piece for next week's paper. Petty, yes, but satisfying.

After drying her hands, she stepped into the small hallway and into Tor Gunnar's chest.

"We have to stop meeting like this," he said wryly.

"Did you follow me?" She pushed off him, aghast. Was her face splotchy?

Just when she'd thought her situation couldn't get worse, leave it to fate to say, "Hold my beer."

"You left your purse on the table." He extended her purse with a stiff arm. "I thought you might want it."

"What?" She didn't have the first clue what thoughts marched through this man's mind.

"I should be asking you that. Were you crying?"

"No. Of course not." She snatched the purse and shoved it under her arm. "It's awesome to hang out with a guy who hates your guts. Super relaxing."

"Hates your . . . what?" he spluttered, glowering at her. "What makes you think I hate you?"

Great. This guy was Mr. Literal. Now she'd get some big speech about how technically he didn't hate her, only disregarded her, and somehow that was even more awful.

She straightened to her whole impressive five feet and a half. "Don't you?"

"Neve." He took a step forward, filling the whole alcove, the clean citrus scent on his skin permeating the air. Her entire world shrank like a deflating helium balloon and the only thing she could do was try to focus, her gaze fixed on the third button of his blue shirt, the one that fastened in the center of his chest. The same chest that was currently heaving as if he'd just completed a record sprint.

Okay, then. He wasn't unaffected by her proximity either.

Sweat misted the valley between her breasts. The soft, worn cotton of her bra was too rough against the sensitive peaks.

She shifted, clenching her thighs together. "Tor, listen—"

"If I hated you, then why would I want to kiss you so damn bad?"

Her heart gave up beating. She wasn't going to survive the heat melting his frosty gaze.

"Kiss me?" Her mouth formed the words, but she wasn't sure if she managed to squeak the question out loud until the corner of his mouth crooked.

"That an invitation?" Wry amusement entered his tone.

And there went the bones in her legs—poof, gone.

The only choice left was to fling her arms out and grip his broad, strong shoulders.

"If you want it to be." Her voice sounded like that of a stranger, a gal who danced burlesque in heels and applied bold lipstick, who could lounge in comfy sweats but also rock a pair of sexy, butt-molding skinny jeans when the fancy struck.

A woman not afraid to reach out and take a little pleasure.

And so . . . just like that . . . she did.

It took Tor's brain a second to register that he was kissing Neve Angel.

He was *kissing* Neve Angel.

No. Scratch that.

He was kissing the shit out of Neve Angel like a motherfucking boss.

While his mind blanked, his body got busy. Mentally, he was still processing that her lips tasted cool, tart and sweet like pink lemonade, while one of his hands dipped around her waist and hauled her against him, and the other found the bathroom door handle and turned. They tumbled inside.

And the real surprise wasn't even that he devoured the glorious heaven that was Neve Angel's mouth. It was that she kissed *him* back. Her tongue stroked his with such sweet fire that his body ignited.

He couldn't decide where to touch first, so like a greedy bastard he tried to get everywhere at once. Her hair was even softer than it looked, but thick and wavy. He coiled his fingers in deep, tugging to turn her head back, intensifying the kiss. She was a thunderclap on a sunny day, a four-leaf clover in a sidewalk crack, hitting every green light the whole drive home. Wholly unexpected. Better than anything he'd ever imagined.

And he'd imagined, all right. Even as he'd tried to push the thoughts away, the fantasies had reeled him back time and time again.

"Neve." Was the word a question or a prayer? All he

knew was it tasted right, like taking a sip of good wine and letting the complex flavors linger on the tongue.

"No more talking," she ordered. Their lips crushed back together, teeth knocking. He skimmed his fingers to where her shirt rode up. When he grazed that sliver of bare, smooth skin, it was like everything in his life made sense, every bit of bad luck or stroke of good fortune had a single purpose—to bring him here. Right here . . . to this moment in a dive-bar bathroom, where he got to explore a perfect landscape of silky skin.

Neve commenced her own explorations, but like with everything else, she was direct—cut right to the chase. He sucked in a rasping breath as she skimmed the bulge in his jeans, pressing her palm flat, the pressure cording the muscles in his neck.

"So much for foreplay," he choked.

She might have snapped "Screw foreplay," but it was drowned out by a loud bang from outside.

"Yo! Did someone fall in and drown?" A deep, drunken voice slurred. "Open up. I've got to take a leak."

And just like that the spell broke. Neve leapt back and her hand flew to cover her mouth, wiping her lips as if removing evidence of his kisses.

He watched her wordlessly as she threw open the door and dove into the noisy bar. How fucking stupid to think that there was anything magic about a frantic hookup in a dingy bar bathroom. This wasn't a happy accident but one giant mistake, which for a moment felt so damn right.

Chapter Seven

"WHAT THE HELL, were you two fuckin' or what?"

"Such a lovely command you have of the English language." Neve grimaced at the frat boy's sour beer breath as he blocked her path from the bathroom, leering from beneath the brim of his white hat. "I'll go with 'or what,' thanks."

"I better not be slipping in no sticky shit." The white hat's wet mouth twisted in a lecherous smirk as he tried focusing over her shoulder. His eyes widened as he noticed who stood behind her. "Hold up . . . Coach? Tor Gunnar, dude. Holy shit, no way, you're a legend."

The dude-bro frat boy pushed past her, literally shoving her out of the way and extending a hand. "Those were some legit plays that last game, man. The lockout blows. Guess you deserve getting a little stinky pinky—"

What fresh hell was this? Neve's throat slammed shut

and she bolted out of the back hall into the throng in the bar. It was like playing the world's worst game of Would You Rather. Would you rather maul your nemesis in The Watering Hole bathroom or hear a frat boy use the words *stinky pinky* in reference to your own vagina?

Two sets of curious eyes watched her approach the table. Breezy and Jed had called a halftime in their round of tonsil hockey. Neve heaved an inward groan. Guess she was supposed to be the entertainment.

"Where's Margot?" she asked, as if she'd merely gone to the bathroom and never in ten million years compiled research about the size and shape of Tor Gunnar's dick.

But if there was one person in the world who was impossible to fool, it was a sister.

"Margot's made a new friend, as per usual." Breezy gestured toward the bar, where Margot sat on the counter, legs swinging, and still whispering to the cute bartender. "But what's up?" Her gaze narrowed. "Your cheeks are red."

"Hey."

Neve stiffened as Tor slid into the seat beside her. She refused to glance over and instead focused on his hand, the one that had just roamed the wilds of her body like Davy Crockett. It sported fresh scrapes on the knuckles, the middle one split.

"Hey! You're bleeding, man," Jed said, passing him a napkin. "What were you doing?"

Tor grabbed a napkin and pressed it to his hand as

Neve's heart skipped a beat. From the corner of her eye she saw the frat boy from the hallway storming to the exit with one eye swollen shut.

"He defended my honor," she broke in wryly, still unable to believe it.

Had Tor really done that? Punched the white-hat asshole?

Breezy and Jed paused before bursting out laughing.

"Good one." Her sister's shoulders shook. "You deadpan better than anyone. For a second I almost believed you."

Breezy didn't mean her amusement to come across as mean. Neve abstractly knew she laughed out of disbelief that Tor would ever be called upon to be her heroic knight in shining armor.

But to a sour, hurting part deep in her soul, it sounded mocking.

The gorgeous head coach of a professional hockey team body checking a drunken frat boy on my behalf? Yeah. Right. Dream on.

"Got my hand jammed in a door while trying to get some air." Tor drained his glass without further explanation.

Such an obvious lie. Confusion swept through her as her brain grappled for any logic. Tor Gunnar *had* punched that jerk. Did he really fight for her? The notion shouldn't be sexy. Violence was never the answer. But— *gah*—there was something so undeniably delicious about a straight-laced man turning into an utter caveman.

But then again, look at the facts. He wasn't giving her a pent-up look full of secret "I shed blood for you" passion. In fact, he stared past her shoulder as if she wasn't even there, like what had happened in that bathroom meant nothing.

As if he'd already forgotten it.

A wave of insecurity swept away any arousal.

"We got a game this weekend, playing Michigan State. Want to come offer some advice?" Jed asked him after a beat.

Neve appreciated her sister's boyfriend's low tolerance for conversational silences. Let him fill the air space and keep the attention off her. And Tor's knuckles.

"Can't. I'm going to a wedding." He made it sound like he was getting a root canal.

"Shouldn't that be a happy occasion?" Margot plonked down, jumping in mid-conversation as usual.

"It's for my ex-wife," Tor said crisply. "I'm sure *she* is looking forward to it."

Neve's mouth dried. He was going to watch his ex-wife marry another man. Eeesh. That *was* on par with getting a root canal. Without novocaine.

"Ouch, that's no bueno." Margot wrinkled her nose. "Hope you've lined up a hot date as a matter of pride."

"I'm flying solo," Tor grunted.

"Are you crazy?" Margot was never one to beat around a bush. "No, no, no! You can't do that. That's a rookie move. Think over your options. Who can you ask? *Someone* has to volunteer as tribute."

"My sister did. Then she fell rock climbing. Unfortunately, her rehabilitation doesn't gel with that timetable." Tor's frosty rebuttal settled over the table like another ice age, freezing them into another awkward silence. Even Margot appeared to be quelled.

"The air-hockey table has opened up." Jed pointed, once again saving the day.

"I'm in," Neve announced, eager for the distraction, just as Tor muttered, "Sounds good."

"Ooh, competition! I like it!" Margot rubbed her hands together. "Let's play battle of the sexes! First round Breezy and Neve versus Tor and Jed."

"Hey now, this isn't going to be fair." Neve hoped her sarcastic drawl hid the fact her nipples could cut glass.

"It's going to be awkward when we school you boys in front of the whole bar," Breezy crowed.

"You're that good, huh?" Tor said patronizingly.

"Not me." Breezy held up her hands and shook her head. "*Her.*"

"I've been hearing for a while that Neve here has mad air-hockey skills." Jed fed a dollar into a machine, nodding to a trio of college girls who snapped his picture before rushing off in a fit of giggles.

Breezy didn't even bat an eye.

"Doesn't that ever bother you?" Neve whispered.

"Nah, why should it? I mean, he *is* gorgeous. Let 'em look." She winked. "I'm the one going home with him at the end of the night."

Neve's laugh felt hollow. Her sister was confident in

her love. So optimistic in his devotion that trust came as easily to her as breathing. No doubt or hesitation. Could love really be like that?

The puck went whizzing by her defenses into the goal.

"Hellions one, Angels zero." Tor smirked. He was back to his usual self, no trace of the passionate man from minutes ago. All cool confidence. Handsome and untouchable. His Scandinavian features were as severe and inscrutable as a Norse god's.

"It's like that, is it?" She dropped her chin and pushed up her sleeves. "That point was a gift."

He rolled his eyes. "That a fact?"

"Stick it on Wikipedia and let it be known."

"All right, trash talkers. Let's sweeten the pot," Margot said, ripping the hair elastic off her wrist and tying her long brown hair up into a ponytail.

"What are we talking about here, a wager?" Jed drawled. "Because I could call in a whole lot of favors."

Breezy blew him a kiss.

Before Neve could say anything that included the words *gag* and *me*, Tor broke in. "The winners get to call in a favor from the losers. One deed."

A few minutes ago she'd played tonsil hockey with this guy. And he hadn't treated her like a cold fish but a triple-layered chocolate-fudge cake. Then he'd ignored her. Now he wanted a favor if she lost? No way.

But at the exact same time, an idea dropped on her head with the force of a cartoon anvil . . . If she won, she could force him to agree to an exclusive no-holds-barred, in-depth profile. Forget the measly top-five article. She'd grill him hard. Figure out what made him tick. Ask nosy questions to her heart's content.

If he wanted to mess with her, she'd mess back.

"Deal," Neve shot back. "As long as it's not illegal."

Jed groaned. "Where's the fun in that?"

"Enough, you." Breezy giggled as if this was some sort of private joke.

Double ew. Neve was happy to let them have their mystery. Some things she just really, really didn't want to know, like what her sister got up to in the boudoir. "Enough chitchat." She set her striker on the table. "Got to be in it to win it."

Because she'd win. Probably. The problem was . . . Breezy sucked at air hockey. She loved her sister, but as she blocked one of Jed's blank shots and pulled back quickly to guard the goal, Neve had to concede the obvious. They were outmatched.

From the sly look in Jed's eyes, it seemed as if he knew exactly what favor he wanted to collect from her sister. And from the erratic, clumsy way Breezy kept trying to score, there was a real and pressing danger that her own teammate might be throwing the game to be in her boyfriend's debt.

But Tor wasn't flirting. Or smiling. He played like a man possessed. She'd never seen him on the ice, at least not in person. There was a chance she'd *once* dredged up some old footage from his Gopher days on YouTube while devouring an entire pint of Cherry Garcia.

But that fact was never to be spoken about, or acknowledged.

She doubled down on the offense, scoring a point, but then Breezy bumped her elbow as she tried to play defense. They were back to being tied for the game point.

"This is it, ladies and gentleman," Margot drawled in a deep, announcer-type voice. "The moment of truth." And she wasn't just hamming it up for her own amusement. A small crowd had gathered, recording the game on their phones. She'd bet five bucks that the majority of these women were focused on capturing shots of Jed West, although to give Coach his credit, he wasn't without his own cadre of female admirers.

"Come on," she snapped to her sister. "Let's get it together."

Her potshot fooled Jed as she tricked him with a fake out by intentionally aiming her shot not into their goal but off the table in front of him, sending the puck back, where she could quickly attack with a rebound.

But Tor, damn it, he was too much of a coach, cataloguing her plays and reviewing her weaknesses. He was ready for the pump fake and stopped it short. Then he struck his mallet hard, sending the puck bouncing off a side wall.

Neve saw it coming. She knew she could stop it. But he played with such a strange intensity that her own curiosity was sparked. If she was in Tor Gunnar's debt, what favor would he request? Her mind screamed *No!* but her body was . . . curious.

And his puck slipped into her goal.

"Oh darn!" Breezy squealed, sounding less than dismayed.

Neve lifted her gaze straight to Tor's. Her cheeks heated. He stared back, a flicker of confusion crossing his face. It had been subtle, but he knew she'd just thrown the game.

But he didn't know why.

And that made two of them. Damn it. She tucked a lock of hair behind her ear and glanced away. She'd just thrown away one heck of a professional coup. And for what?

He'd likely humiliate her in some way. What would it be . . .? Stroll down 16th Ave. dressed in a tutu? Go to a karaoke bar and sing "Don't Stop Believing"?

"Good game," Margot said as they filed back into their booth. "Now the winners get to call in the debt. This should be interesting."

"That's one word for it," Jed said.

"Stop," Breezy pleaded in a giddy tone that made it clear they had about two more minutes before she asked to close the tab and run home.

"Inquiring minds want to know." Neve addressed her comment to Tor, even as she studied her drink. "What's it going to be? I know my pride is about to take a beating so let's get the suspense over with." Her stomach felt so tense that there was no way she'd risk a sip at this point. The last thing she needed to do was choke at the table.

Or get more mouth to mouth from the coach.

"I thought it over and you are all right. I can't go to my ex's wedding alone." Tor's tone was pure confident arrogance, even as he drummed his index finger on the table.

Neve's body didn't have time to release a flood of adrenaline before she was hit with the second part of his statement.

"Since you lost, Neve, you'll go with me. Two days in Telluride. Ever been?"

"I- I had friends go there for music festivals while I was at college, but I always stayed behind to do summer school," she managed to stammer, trying to comprehend the magnitude of what he just said.

"Then it's a date. I'll send you the details."

"A . . . date," Neve repeated blankly.

He nodded once, a dare in his eyes.

Whisky. Tango. Foxtrot. Her stomach did its best impersonation of an amusement-park log ride and splashed down to her toes.

Because no matter how much she wanted to pretend, she couldn't fake that the kiss in the bathroom hadn't felt oh, so real. He might be setting her up for a fall, but she couldn't quite stop herself from tiptoeing to the edge.

She needed to keep her head in the game. Look for the opportunity. After all, for better or worse, she'd be alone, more or less, for a weekend with Tor Gunnar, the biggest enigma in NHL coaching, and she'd figure out what made him tick at last—by hook or crook.

She couldn't wait to tell Scott about the trip. This was just the kind of opportunity that would cause her editor to freak out.

When life handed her lemons, she made delicious lemonade.

Two deep lines materialized between his brows—at least he had the good sense to look concerned.

"Game on," she said blithely, picking up her drink and giving him a toast. "After all, I've never been over to Telluride. It will be an . . . adventure." Perfect. She'd swashbuckled through his little dare with expert precision. All the points to her.

You don't scare me, Tor Gunnar.

She took a long swallow of the margarita, the frozen slush sluicing over her front teeth and creating one heck of a brain freeze. Try as she might, she couldn't hold back a wince, because all her tough talk sat on a throne of lies. Tor Gunnar might not scare her, but the unfathomable expression in his eyes sure as heck did.

He had an agenda. She needed to figure out what it was for her own sanity.

Chapter Eight

_____

TOR SAT, DISORIENTED. The clock beside his bed read three in the morning. Looked like he'd fallen asleep after all. The way he'd tossed and turned after the bar, he'd figured it would be another one of those restless nights where he watched the sun rise.

The phone ring registered in his sleep-drunk brain.

"Shit." He sprang into action. His first thought was Olive. But the number on the screen was unfamiliar. One of the guys?

"Hello?" he said, frowning.

"It's stupid to call, but I can't sleep. I need to know why. Why'd you do it?"

The familiar woman's voice jolted him like a triple-shot espresso. "Neve?"

"Do you enjoy messing with me, is that it?" Her tone was strained. "Because I've been going over tonight's events with a fine-tooth comb and nothing adds up. I mean, you went and ate my face after informing my colleagues that I was a cold fish. Then you rearranged that dumbass frat boy's face after he insulted me. And *then* the coup de grace . . . an invite to a weekend away in Telluride? For your wife's wedding?"

"She is my ex-wife," he bit back. "Very much *ex*."

"Still . . . color me confused, Coach."

"What's so hard to understand?" He kicked off the comforter and eased back against his headboard. A shaft of moonlight shone on the end of the bed; if he reached out he'd be able to touch it. "Who knows? Maybe I'm interested in getting to know you more."

"Good story. Except does the phrase 'fuck a penguin' ring a bell?"

Shit. He'd said that. And the stupid cold fish comment. Both were knee-jerk reactions designed to deflect attention from the truth . . . that he couldn't get enough of this maddening woman. He'd acted like a middle school doofus, teasing the girl he crushed on.

He wasn't proud.

"All I can guess is that you must enjoy torturing your enemies."

"Was kissing me torture?" His cock stirred in his boxer briefs at the memory.

"Don't fuck around, Gunnar."

"Nice mouth you've got."

She made a choking sound. "Pot meet kettle."

"I'll be honest. I *am* interested, all right? I think you

know that though. I think you've always known. And what's more . . . I think you might be curious too."

Silence dragged. For a second he wondered if she'd hung up. Maybe he was reading this all wrong.

"Well . . . this is an unexpected direction."

"I'm full of surprises." He raked a hand through his hair. The darkness made him honest. "But here's more truth. I'm glad you agreed to come to the wedding. I'm glad you said yes."

"It can't be an easy event." She cleared her throat. "I mean, you loved your ex, right?"

"Once upon a time. But it wasn't a fairy tale. We've been co-parents for years and it's Olive who wants me there."

"Your daughter."

"She's ten." Not many things made him smile on demand, but Olive always did. "And I don't want you worrying about logistics. We'll have separate rooms. I've already called the hotel. I'm not looking to take advantage of you."

"I see," she replied, sounding a little confused. He didn't blame her. Nor was he being entirely truthful.

Their chemistry was undeniable. Hell yes he wanted to take advantage. He wanted to take her every which way and twice on Sunday.

"What's the game plan? We drive down this weekend?"

"Yeah." He cleared his throat. "It'll take seven hours. The valley is an out-of-the-way pain in the ass to get to. But believe me, the San Juan Mountains are something to see."

"I'm Colorado born and raised and have never spent much time in the ski towns. It was too expensive for my family when I was a kid, and now my winters are too busy for vacations."

He sighed, smile fading. "Mine too."

"What have you been doing since the lockout?"

"Watching tapes." His mouth flattened. "Reviewing plays. Climbing the walls. You?"

"Yesterday I wrote yet another lockout think piece, *blech*. Then I tried learning to knit off YouTube. I'm making a pot holder . . . I think. Or a lap blanket for a guinea pig."

"Pot holder." He tried and failed to picture her in the kitchen, being domestic. "You cook?"

"No. Ew. I barely toast bread." She gave a short self-deprecating laugh. "But circle back to the lockout for a second. Are there any rumors floating around about negotiations—please say we're close to a deal?"

He stiffened. "No." The easiness from a moment ago disappeared, the question a reminder that she wasn't NeverL8, a woman he'd flirted harmlessly with online. This was Neve Angel and any slip of the tongue could have real and lasting career consequences. He couldn't forget she was a journalist, and he was playing with fire.

"I'm not fishing," she said testily. "I didn't call you at three in the morning to try and trick you out of insider NHL information, if that's what you're thinking."

"I wasn't." He massaged an ache spreading across his forehead. "I'm not."

"You're a good kisser, but a terrible liar, Tor Gunnar. But it doesn't matter because whatever game you're playing, I'm going to win." And that was when she did hang up.

Tor groaned and dropped his phone off the side of the bed before bracing his face in his hands. How were they going to spend the entire weekend together and not commit murder?

And out of all the women in the entire fucking world, why was she the one who made him come alive?

Since his divorce, he'd been frozen. He didn't miss feeling that he was always disappointing someone, that he was never enough. Maddy used to cry in the shower, where she thought he couldn't hear. But each and every time he'd go stand by the door, put his hand on the knob and tell himself to open it, to go inside and see what was eating at her.

But he'd been too chicken shit.

At work he'd he always had a game plan and the right answer. Coaching made sense. He was good at it in a way he'd never been as a spouse.

Yeah, he might have been a better husband than his Pop. He didn't yell or get drunk, and he'd hack off his arm before raising it against a woman. But that didn't mean he knew the first thing about how to be a significant other, as that disastrous phone call just confirmed.

He knew how to be a father. He knew how to be a friend. He knew how to be a coach. But he was clueless how to prevent himself from driving a lover away, giving them no chance but to end things on their own. His reticence wasn't about a fear of commitment. He wanted someone to nestle beside in the darkest nights, to know what they ate for breakfast, how they took their coffee, to give and receive love.

He rolled over in his empty bed and flung an arm across his forehead. But it had always been easier to push women away, so he didn't know what the hell to do about this strange pull toward Neve.

Or if he could do better this time and not screw everything up.

"NEED HELP?" THE shop assistant chirped.

Talk about a loaded question. Because yes, Neve needed help. Lots of help on multiple levels. But she'd rather freeze her tongue to a flagpole before admitting as much. "No." She issued one of her tight "back away slowly" smiles. "I'm fine."

"Are you looking for any particular occasion?" This redheaded assistant wasn't giving up easily.

"A wedding." Her curt tone disinvited further questions but the girl still seemed undeterred. Neve tucked her chin and walked self-consciously toward a little black dress on a center rack. That could work. Timeless elegance. A little Audrey Hepburn. And after all, black was her color.

"Aw, love a wedding!" The woman sounded like she meant it too. "Who is the happy couple? Friend? Sister? Brother?"

"The ex-wife to my date," she answered crisply, leaving out the part where she was also going to commit espionage and root out her archenemy's secrets and win whatever secret game he played.

"Ohhhhhh." The assistant's eyes rounded just a bit. "This is a challenge. You have to look gooood."

Neve stiffened. "What do you mean?"

"Your date is taking you to his ex-wife's wedding. Wow. That means he's showing you off."

Neve pressed a hand to her chest. "Me?"

Her confusion was met with a sage nod. "You're a statement. The evidence he's got a chance at his own happy ending. And you need a dress that's going to make a splash."

"Yeah, about that." Neve's shoulders curled in as she took in the assistant's tiger-print heels. "I'm not really a statement kind of a gal."

"Let's see." The woman gave her a critical appraisal. "I know just the thing. Follow me."

Neve trailed after, too flustered to argue. Tor wasn't bringing her to show her off or out of interest. He probably wanted to make a fool out of her.

"Yes, this. This is perfect." The assistant pulled out a short, intricate scalloped-lace dress in a rich greenish-blue hue.

"But . . . it's so feminine." Neve was scared to even touch it. The color *was* beautiful, vibrant and lush but classy. If she wore a dress like that she'd be noticed, not as a tough-as-nails reporter but as a sexy woman.

And that thought terrified her.

But another powerful thought took root. She'd like to see Tor try not be tempted by her in this dress.

"With your dark hair and those eyes, and that mouth. Dear lord, your poor date. It's just not fair. He won't be able to take his eyes off you." The assistant swung the dress beneath Neve's chin and tittered.

Neve stared at herself in the mirror, taking in the unforced compliments and imagining herself wearing it. Misgivings waged a final last stand. "This isn't my usual style."

"It should be," the assistant responded firmly. "You have such bold, classic features. You can pull it off."

There was no doubt the color suited her. Neve would never have thought in a million years to pick something so bright.

"And remember, you want to keep the makeup simple. With your complexion, that shouldn't be a problem. You have lashes to die for . . . Are they natural? And can we talk about your eyebrows? Because yes. So much yes."

"You mean bushy." She hated to give voice to her deeply private insecurities. It was so much easier to march around life pretending to be ultra-confident. But what the hell, sometimes honesty was the best policy.

"Those brows are fierce. We're talking *Vogue* eyebrows; people pay good money trying to get them. I'm not kidding. There are Facebook ads for eyebrow wigs on my timeline at least once a week. Wear the dress, let

your hair down and do loose finger curls, and then treat
yourself to a really killer shade of lipstick."

"Lipstick?"

"Oh, honey." The assistant's wince didn't hurt as much
when she rolled her head to one side and gave a kind
smile. "I'm going to hit you with some real talk. You're
getting this dress aaaand a few lacey things in our under-
garment area. Then I want you to head across the street
to that shop over there." She pointed out the window at
a makeup boutique. "Ask for Sally. She's a friend of mine.
Tell her that Kendall sent you and she's to hook you up
with Inner Diva."

"Inner what?"

"Trust me, it's a lipstick that is bright red with a blue
undertone. Perfect for your alabaster skin."

"I think you mean *pasty*."

"Hun, no, no, no. Stop this all right now. This is a No
Negative Self-Talk Zone. You've got to be unapologeti-
cally your own gorgeous self," she chided.

What a unique idea.

"Remember that you are perfect in every imperfec-
tion. Now come take a look at these garter belts."

The muscles in her throat constricted. "Garter belts?"
Well, then. It looked as if she was well and truly crawling
out of her rut. If she took away her limits, there was no
telling how far she could go.

At least one thing was certain: She'd go into this
weekend guns blazing.

Tor Gunnar better hang on to his hat.

Chapter Nine

LIFE COULD BE one fickle bitch. For months Tor had dreaded attending Maddy's wedding, but ever since Neve agreed to be his plus-one, the days had crept by at the pace of a narcoleptic snail. No cure existed for this level of restless agitation, except work. With the lockout showing no signs of letting up, he resorted to taking long, punishing runs along the High Line Canal, but even that lung-busting exercise brought limited relief. Same went for the trips to the racquet-ball court. His sanity—and body—were taking one hell of a beating.

Speaking of beating—best to ignore the fact that his morning shower routine now included a mandatory jack-off session . . . with a certain dark-eyed sports journalist serving as muse during the grand finale.

But the day had finally arrived. In seven hours, he'd

be pulling into Telluride Valley with Neve Angel sitting shotgun.

His head rocked back as he swallowed a groan. This was how Superman must feel when staring down a pile of kryptonite. When it came to trying to squelch his attraction for that woman, he was fucking powerless.

He mulled over the upcoming day's game plan while finishing packing. Not much space would separate them inside his Porsche—a foot at best. And she'd smell damn good. Fresh-cut grapefruit sprinkled with a pinch of sugar. During those stolen moments back at The Watering Hole last week, he'd breathed in her shampoo's crisp citrus zest. The memory of that scent still clung to him, tangy and addictive. He had to be strong, ready to brace for that sweet assault and the "getting to know you" small talk that rubbed his mind like sandpaper.

Strange how this woman had orbited in his sphere for years, and yet he hardly knew anything about her apart from the byline.

Hockey. The idea shot into his head with lightning-bolt force. *Of course.* Yes. *Jesus.* It was so obvious. They'd discuss hockey. Neve Angel loved her job. That much was never in doubt. And they shared a love for the game. Their strong work ethic could serve as common ground, except—he frowned—that whole part where her life's work apparently relied on her being a thorn in his side.

Scratch any idea about discussing work and steer to neutral ground. Back to the drawing board. Music made for a good Switzerland, and he owned a shit ton of music. If she was a Springsteen fan, they'd be in business. He owned every track The Boss had ever laid down.

He could crank *Nebraska* or *The River* and hope for the best. Not the wiliest strategy ever devised, but it might cloak the fact he was uncertain on his positioning and plays.

Striding into his walk-in closet, he selected two dress shirts off the hangers, the light blue and a darker navy one. After folding and packing both, he shut the lid to his suitcase. Fuck it, no point stewing. Besides, the drive into the mountains was just the beginning of the adventure. On Sunday afternoon, they'd have to make the return journey, and then there was the matter of the hours between . . . and the two nights in the same hotel.

Although not the same room. He'd share a double-bed suite with his daughter, Olive, while Neve was safely sequestered down the hall. Out of reach. Out of trouble.

He rolled his shoulders and cracked his neck. Separate rooms. Safe. Yes, good. It wasn't like they were going to get naked.

The image of naked Neve appeared unbidden in his mind's eye. Her small body, lithe and sleek, shining like pale moonlight while a feline smile curled the corners of her mouth. It didn't take much brainpower to imagine all the things that might make her purr.

The air in his lungs went as shallow as the water in a kiddie pool. Getting a deep breath was nothing but an exercise in wishful thinking. Rocked by a wave of dizziness, he snapped the suitcase locks shut and braced his hands on top of the lid, taking a moment to regroup.

Note to self: Do not picture Neve Angel naked unless wishing to invite a full-scale panic attack.

This lust-filled distraction was unfamiliar territory. He wasn't a guy who lost his shit over a woman. He'd seen this kind of thing happen to other guys but had never gone there in real life. Not even with Maddy.

If he was going to survive the weekend with his sanity intact, he'd need to start using the head located on top of his neck, not just his buddy south of the border.

Although—he chewed his lower lip, pondering—as a purely hypothetical exercise, would the idea of stripping Neve down to her smile send her running for the nearest mountain? He glanced at himself. He wore his usual outfit: polished brown loafers, khakis, navy sweater and a sport jacket. No woman had seen him naked in a long time—years—but all was in working order.

"Working order?" He spat out the thought. "Jesus Christ, Gunnar." He grabbed his suitcase and stormed out to his garage. He was head coach for a two-time-champion professional hockey team and had no game. What a joke. The world should be his oyster, and here he was, acting allergic to shellfish.

He needed to nut up and calm down. After throwing the suitcase into the Porsche trunk, he climbed behind the wheel and turned on Byways to navigate. Neve had texted him her address this morning without any accompanying "Looking forward to the weekend!" Or even a generic smiley face. Not one single message expressing interest or excitement for the journey ahead.

An auspicious start.

He started the engine and backed out. Sweating about their upcoming proximity was pointless. He'd made his bed, and Neve wouldn't be lying in it, clothed or otherwise. He had forced her into an awkward situation by insisting she serve as his date to his ex's wedding. Not exactly the kind of romantic gesture that made a woman swoon. But there was no going back. No way out of the next forty-eight hours but through.

He idled at a red light. A dead leaf swirled through the air and skimmed across the gleaming black hood. A shadow of doubt darkened his mood. This weekend was only happening due to an impulsive game of air hockey. It wasn't like she *wanted* to come.

But then . . . he'd never forced Neve to take an oath signed in blood and notarized by the devil. She'd lost a friendly bet, and if she didn't want to come, she could have refused. So seeing as she *was* open to coming along for the ride . . . maybe she felt the same spark. Or at least a curious flicker.

Or maybe this was her chance to torment him in some fresh new way. Suspicion gripped him once more.

The ugly truth was that either option was just as likely as the other. He wanted to play with fire, and she was a book of matches. No telling what might burn down between them.

When he reached her town house, she was already waiting outside on the curb, perched on her suitcase beneath a bare oak. Head bent, her face was shielded by an inky curtain of hair. When she raised her head, he sucked in a sharp breath. Here was a face that was impossible to judge at first glance. For too many, a quick glance at Neve might not afford much reward. But for those who made an effort, the payoff was huge.

Her looks weren't easy, nothing fragile or cute on offer. Each of her features was as strong as a shot of whisky, not unlike the woman herself. Truth be told, part of what intoxicated him about her was that intangible air of toughness.

He wasn't a soft, easy man. And she didn't look like she'd break at the first sign of trouble.

"Hey!" She stood, cheeks pink from the crisp air.

"Hello," he said after clearing his throat, trying like hell not to focus on the way the autumn sun reflected off her hair. Instead, he got out and went for her bag; more useful and a hell of a lot easier than making continued eye contact.

"Hey, it's cool. I can get that." She reached for the bag handle.

"I know," he said, not releasing his grip. "But there is this new thing that I'm trying."

She frowned a little, cocking her head. "Which is . . .?"

"Trying to be nicer," he muttered in a gruff undertone.

That seemed to give her food for thought. "To me or in general?"

Sassy thing. "You, but got to say, Angel, you don't make it easy."

She stared boldly as he picked up the suitcase, refusing to blink first. Her hair was different this morning, down and soft around her face. And her white puffy jacket enhanced her dark hair and red lips—making for an arresting combination of Snow White and Lisbeth Salander from *The Girl with the Dragon Tattoo*.

"You're wearing lipstick," he observed, opening up the passenger door for her.

"So?" Her hand flew up as if to hide the evidence.

She was jumpy as a grasshopper in June. "Simmer down. So nothing." He frowned. What had he said wrong now? "I'm just making a simple observation."

"Yeah right." The faintest trace of a snort.

By the time he'd walked around the front of the car, climbed inside and jammed his key into the ignition, nervous anticipation filled him to the brim. He had to play this exactly right or he was going to slosh shit over the side and make a mess of everything. "I said something wrong." He waited a second. "What was it?"

"Nothing." She waved one hand before plucking some invisible string from her denim-clad knee, a moment of vulnerability flickering across her face. "At least not technically. I just . . . Gah. It's stupid. But please don't tease me about makeup."

Her surprise admission momentarily stunned him into silence. "I'm not following your train of thought."

"Forget about it," she said, mouth mashing into a hard line. "That's not what I'm asking."

Okay. He didn't speak woman, but something was definitely off. "I wasn't teasing you, Neve." He spoke her name with intention, wanting her to hear him. "Wear lipstick. Or don't. What do I care? You look good either way. But I'm allowed to notice you. Making an observation doesn't necessarily make me an asshole."

She huffed a sigh. "You're right."

She's shy.

The realization caught him by surprise. It was like peeking through a brick wall, and inside was a strange and beautiful garden.

"Hey. Listen up. I've got a proposal." He turned and met her gaze straight on, elbow propped on the console. "What if we declare a truce for the weekend?"

Out of any of the millions of combinations of words he could have uttered, he appeared to have found the ones able to render her speechless. "Truce?" she repeated at last.

"Just until we get back and then you can return to your regularly scheduled loathing."

"I don't loathe you . . ." Her mouth slid into a half grin. "At least not all the time."

"Hey, I get it." He shrugged and started the car, the six-cylinder engine purring like a jungle cat. "For what it's worth, Rovhal means *asshole* in Swedish. I'm third generation. My grandparents were farmers outside Älmhult."

"Sorry, I'm not up to speed on Scandinavian geography."

"In the south, not far from Denmark. Home of the first IKEA store."

"For real?" That got her attention. "What a claim to fame."

"There's a museum."

"What's there?" She grinned. "Displays of flat packs with unfathomable names? Shrines to cheap Swedish meatballs?"

His brow creased. "I never went. My father wasn't one for nostalgia . . . at least not until the end of his life."

"Ah," she said lightly, as if sensing they skated over conversational thin ice. "Well, at least that solves the mystery of Rovhal. I'd wondered." She reached out a hand and when he shook it her palm was warm, her fingers soft, even as her shake was firm. "Nice to officially meet you, Rovhal. Since all is being revealed, mind cluing me in on what the 30 stands for?"

"My lucky number." He didn't release her hand as he made his confession. "That's how old I was when I had my daughter. She's the best thing that's ever happened to me."

"What a . . . lovely thing to say." She blinked in surprise, as if seeing him for the first time. "All right, then. To a truce." Neve glanced to their interlocking fingers and then back up. "At least for the next two days. Telluride or bust."

"Thank you for coming with me," he said quietly. "I . . . didn't want to go alone."

Silence fell. "I won't tell anyone," she said at last, slowly withdrawing her hand. "Or the fact that unlike your alter ego suggests, you aren't a totally awful person. Who knows, I might have just made the discovery of the century. Tor Gunnar might be a good guy."

"I like that level of optimism, Angel."

"Thanks, Coach." But her snort didn't appear unkind. Her gaze was cautious, but also curious.

As if she wondered about him, as much as he wondered about her.

He made good time getting out of the city despite the morning traffic. It didn't take long until he had them cruising southwest on US 285. But it soon became obvious that despite their agreement to a cessation in hostilities, the drive wasn't going to be full of warm fuzzies. Any of his initial strained questions were met with monosyllabic answers.

Time for plan B. Operation Saved by Springsteen. He cranked up the stereo and focused on "Born to Run." But despite the music, an unsettled quiet took root and spread. His heart beat in time to the melody. His shoulders tensed.

He was trying his best and didn't know how to steer them back on track. Neve had hunched in on herself, shoulders stooped. Didn't so much as glance his direction, or even straight ahead. Her hand splayed on the passenger-side window as if she wished she was anywhere else. This was it. His worst nightmare. They drove past deep, dramatic canyons and up along the winding road lined with ghostly aspen. He could barely register the scenery. Hard to focus on anything when his heart was going as cold as the surrounding alpine tundra.

Time to reconcile the truth. Wanting something didn't make it happen. This was a terrible idea, the trip a bust before it even began. As much as it would have sucked to attend Maddy's wedding solo, it was going to suck a magnitude of an order worse to bring along an unwilling guest.

"My ears popped." Neve spoke for the first time in an hour as they crested Monarch Pass. The highest point of the drive.

"Not surprised." He cleared his throat, his voice rough with pent-up tension. "We're at 11,312 feet."

His sharp answer got her attention. She turned to face him dead on. "How do you know that so precisely?"

He forced a tight smile and pointed at the road sign. "I can read."

MONARCH PASS: 11,312 FEET. CONTINENTAL DIVIDE.

"Oh." She put her hands on her cheeks and rubbed slow circles under both eyes. "Sorry. I'm a little out of it."

"Is the altitude bothering you? We'll start dropping now all the way into Gunnison, but Telluride still sits at close to nine thousand." He slowed, dropping into Third with a slight frown. He'd been so in his head that he hadn't stopped to study her. Now that he did, she didn't look all that good. She was always pale, but her coloring seemed off, almost grey.

She made a sound that might be a grunt of "Don't worry about it" but could also be a soft moan.

Shit. Something *was* wrong.

He pulled into the empty parking lot for a scenic mountain tram—closed for the winter—and yanked the hand brake. "What's up? You're not feeling okay, are you?" Once they got to Telluride, he could take her to the clinic and get her a prescription written for an oxygen concentrator. Most Colorado ski towns had rental companies as altitude sickness was so common for visitors.

"I'm not too hot." She mashed her lips. "It's cold out but mind if I open the window? At least for a moment. See if that helps settle my stomach?"

"You're carsick?" Everything fell into place. The strained silence. Her rigid posture. "Why didn't you say anything? I would have pulled over." He'd been torturing her for hours without the first clue what was wrong. He'd been so fixated by his worst fears that he hadn't considered the most reasonable solution. Relief and frustration hit him in equal measure.

"It always happens. Since I was a kid. Breezy used to call me Nauseous Neve whenever we had to drive more than a half hour. I didn't want to make a big deal about it to you. I dosed with some motion sickness meds before leaving. They are making me woozy but otherwise that's about it."

His chest thawed. "Is that why you haven't been talking."

"Yup." Her laugh was queasy. "What's your excuse?"

He thought it over and decided to go with honesty. "Social awkwardness."

She grimaced or smiled. Hard to tell under the conditions.

He felt like the biggest dumbshit. She had been sick on his watch and he'd had his head implanted straight up his ass. The urge to fix the situation took over. He'd do better, starting now. "I've got more water in the back."

He went to the trunk, opened a small cooler and grabbed her a bottle, plus the sandwiches that he'd made last night when insomnia made sleep impossible. He grabbed an armload of supplies and got back inside the Porsche.

She stared at the sandwich after he handed one over.

"What is this?" The cellophane baggie crackled between her fingers.

"Nothing fancy. Just plain turkey and cheese." He hesitated. "You aren't a vegetarian, are you?"

"No . . . I just . . ." She blinked. "You made me a sandwich?"

"Is that bad?" Why was she looking at him as if he'd just sprouted horns? All he'd done was take some sourdough bread, slap down turkey and Kraft, smear a little mayo.

She glanced to the sandwich and then back up at him. "It's . . . unexpectedly cute. Tor Gunnar made me a turkey sandwich."

"Cute?" He didn't know what t she was so impressed by, but not going to lie, he liked the fact he'd scored a win. "Got to say, I'm not used to hearing those words directed at me, especially from you."

"Trust me, I'm not used to thinking them." She fiddled with her seat belt, studying the panoramic mountain scenery, and sighed. "This place really is out-of-control beautiful. I need to get out more."

Tor was undeterred by her attempt to deflect and change the subject. "I thought you weren't talking to me because you had second thoughts."

"Look." She glanced over with an uncertain expression. "Let's promise each other one thing, okay? In addition to a truce."

"I'm all ears," he said gruffly.

"There is enough crap in the world without us shoveling more on the pile, don't you think?" The wind blowing in through the cracked-open windows was cold. There was already a few inches of snow dusting the ground even though it had been a drier autumn.

Her coloring improved and she managed a few bites of the sandwich. "You going to answer?" she asked, covering a hand over her mouth, half-filled with food. "Or sit and stare?"

It was damn hard to give words to his truth, to let down his guard and speak from the heart. That he liked this feeling he got watching her eat his simple food. It was nice to feel like he was taking care of her in some small way. "You're right. I'm just glad that you feel better. No crap."

"Good. And can we discuss the magical Tor-turkey-sandwich carsick cure?" Her face softened into a rueful smile. "You could infomercial this. It's amazing how much better I feel. No offense, but I wouldn't have thought this would work in a million years."

"Sometimes magic happens in unlikely places." And from the startled glance she cast him, he knew they were talking about more than unusual home remedies.

THE ADELINE WAS a redbrick boutique hotel nestled in the heart of Telluride's picturesquely historic downtown. Neve took a moment to soak in the updated but undeniably Old West vibe—John Wayne meets modern-day luxury. It was a hundred-year-old brothel given a fashionable new life.

"Let's get our rooms. Let you rest for a bit," Tor said as they walked into the lobby, a cozy and inviting space with pressed-tin ceilings and stuffed leather sofas.

Since Monarch Pass he'd been gravely solicitous, ensuring the windows were cracked and making frequent stops at various scenic pullouts. He might have a hard outer shell, but she couldn't help but wonder what softness hid behind that tough exterior. Just because he wasn't loquacious didn't mean he didn't communicate.

As the hours passed she'd found herself becoming more attuned to the little things, the nuanced expressions on his face when he glanced her way or when a certain song came on. His little quirks and gestures that showed he enjoyed her presence.

Or at least didn't actively dislike it.

It was strange, and disorienting, drawing closer to this standoffish man, breathing in the same air, inhaling the faint cedar and pine undernotes from his aftershave, wondering if maybe she didn't know him at all.

He'd Mr. Darcy dissed her in the stadium parking lot, but maybe she was Elizabeth Bennet-ing him with all of her prejudice. There was so much toxic masculinity in the world that sometimes it was hard to remember that good guys existed.

"Daddy! Daddy! You're here!" A cry cut through the lobby chatter as a wiry girl with braces sprinted across the room and leapt into his arms. She was in that ephemeral stage between child and teen, but one glance at her ice-blue eyes and blond hair made it obvious whose child she was.

Tor's face transformed into an expression Neve had never seen. Complete happiness.

"Hey, baby girl," he said, spun his daughter around twice and then planted a quick kiss on her forehead. "You beat us. I didn't think you were arriving until dinner."

She giggled, adjusting her braid. "I rode up in Aunt

Amber's minivan. She said that I can sleep with Lane and Page. Can I, please? They have connecting rooms with a door to Aunt Amber."

"Your cousins?" He frowned with mock severity. "You sure you won't just be awake talking all night? Remember the last time they came over to my house?"

She was the picture of innocence. "What? It was fine."

"There was that incident with the marshmallows. And the microwave. And the—"

"Pleeeeeeease, pleeeeeeeeasee. We'll be good this time." Olive broke off from her begging to take stock of Neve standing beside him.

"Oh. Hi." Her smile broadened. "You're Neve? He said you had bangs. I like them."

"Uh, yeah," she responded, thrown off balance by the same blue eyes that haunted her dreams in a smaller, perky face. Of course, Tor must have told his daughter she was coming, but she had been so wrapped up in what this trip meant for her that she hadn't fully thought through what it would be like for *him*. The fact that this crowd was made up of people from his life, and he was giving her a backstage pass into what made him tick. For all his mistrust of the press, that was a big gesture.

The evidence was mounting that Tor had no sinister agenda. And the biggest scoop of a story might be that he liked her.

A feeling vibrated through her chest like thunder.

He might like her a lot.

Olive wrapped her arm around Tor's waist and leaned into him, assessing her with an appraising look Neve knew all too well. "Daddy told me all about you."

"Did he, now?" Neve was used to hearing Tor Gunnar called Coach, of course, and less savory things—mostly insults muttered under her own breath—but to hear his daughter speak of him with such bright affection gave her pause.

When he glanced down at his daughter, there was nothing reserved in his face. He looked like any amused father who was slightly skeptical about what his precocious child might say next.

"I *will* be good." Olive shot her father a quick mischievous look. "He made me promise to go easy on you."

"Is that a fact?" Neve placed a hand on one hip. She had limited experience dealing with children and didn't want to make a misstep.

"I ask a lot of questions."

"Me too, as long as it's a day ending in *y*," Neve answered. At least they had something in common. "I look forward to your interrogations."

"Sounds good." Olive laughed, turning back to Tor and batting her lashes. "But, Daddy, seriously, can I share a hotel room with my cousins? I've never done it and I am bigger and I will be good. Please, please please? I'm dying to. Dying, I say."

"Let's go have a word with your aunt. I'll be right back." He gave Neve a curt nod. "If you'll excuse us a moment."

"By all means." Neve gaped as Tor walked over to a gorgeous blonde who was drinking a glass of wine by the roaring fire. While it was fascinating to glean insight into Tor's life, she was also going to smack into his past. A past that was striding into the lobby in a pair of impossibly elegant heeled winter boots and with a delicate heart-shaped face framed by lustrous blond hair that would make Rapunzel weep.

Neve remembered her face from the article she'd written on his divorce, one of her first at the *Age*.

Maddy gave Tor a stiff embrace, air-kissing both of his cheeks. Neve chewed the inside of her lower lip. He'd been married to an air-kisser?

The beautiful woman spoke with animation, twin lines of concern creasing her high, smoo forehead, and as if on some unspoken cue, they both spun and stared in her direction. Neve tried not to grimace. She was so busted, she couldn't even pretend to be inspecting the large Thanksgiving-themed cornucopia on the mantel.

It was obvious she'd been taking in every word.

"Neve?" Impossibly marvelous Maddy took off like an elegant rocket, speeding in her direction. "Hello," she said in a breathy, sleepy voice, as if she'd just woken up from a delicious nap. "Wonderful to meet you. I'm Maddy, Tor's . . . well . . . the bride. Look, there has been just a teensy, tiny mix-up. The hotel is overbooked and when I saw Tor had reserved the extra room, I assumed it was a mistake. My Great Aunt Agnes has settled into what was evidently supposed to be your room and she's ninety-one and. . ." She threw up her hands in a frazzled gesture. "For Pete's sakes. You know what they say about assuming . . ."

"No! N-no, it's fine. You must have a million and one things to think about. Don't give me a second thought," Neve stammered. "Let's leave Aunt Agnes right where she is."

Brave words as her stomach lurched.

She and Tor Gunnar were going to be sharing a hotel room alone for an entire weekend. And she had a suitcase packed with very new and very, very tiny French lingerie.

Chapter Ten

"NICE BED, EMPHASIS on the singular," Neve dead-panned, dropping her suitcase onto the hardwood floor with a dull thud. The impact echoed the crash of his heart against his rib cage.

The room was a blend of rustic and modern. The stuffed chair by the window looked like an inviting place to curl up with a book, while the framed photographs of wildflowers gave the room a touch of feminine whimsy. But there was no denying the space was dominated by the pine-framed king-sized bed.

Perfect for sprawling like a starfish and taking a long winter's nap.

Or trying to medal in the Sexual World Championships.

His mouth filled with invisible sand, going drier

than the Sahara. It was impossible to look anywhere else. Was Neve really going to crawl up onto that giant mattress, her body next to his? He blazed so hot it was a wonder he didn't turn to flame. He set his own bag by the dresser, half expecting to see smoke rippling off the back of his hand.

The light-canceling drapes were long and dark, and he flung them open, needing head space.

"Wow. There's a sight," Neve whispered.

Above them rose the soaring mountains that framed the valley's box canyon, snow blanketing the rust-colored peaks, aspen forests devoid of leaves, gleaming like bone. A frozen waterfall hung suspended off a cliff. Maybe, just maybe, an avalanche would trigger right now and extinguish this mad hope.

"Another mistake. There were supposed to be two beds," he said stiffly before she could accuse him of masterminding a hookup. It had been a while, but he'd never press his advantage.

"I'm not great at math but . . ."

"Shit." His mouth dried at her teasing tone and he spun around, defensively raking a hand through his hair. "I feel like I brought you into a mess. First the shared room, now . . . this . . ." He waved his hand at the thick mattress that looked capable of handling the urgent thrusts of even the longest dry spell.

She didn't look over. Frown lines bracketed her mouth as she reached out and touched the comforter as if it were dangerous. "Well, I'll tell you what. After that drive, we need a drink and a nap."

"I never nap."

"Neither do I." She shrugged off his glare. "But you just drove seven hours. And I spent six of them feeling fifty shades of warmed-over death. So I don't want to stress over Bedgate. I do want to pop open that minibar, treat myself to a stiff drink and pass out until I wake up feeling vaguely human."

"A plan that I can get behind. Two highballs coming right up." He leapt into action and opened the fridge, peering inside. "Vodka. Check. Ginger ale. Check. We can pretend it's a Moscow Mule."

"It could be a Moscow Donkey Surprise and I'd be perfectly content."

"You're on." It was exactly what he needed, a task. There were two tumblers on the desk. "I'll show you a trick I learned on the road. Hold on a second." After scooping them up, he went into the hallway, filled them with ice cubes from the closest machine and came back in. Neve sat on the edge of the bed, legs dangling, feet not quite touching the ground.

Her smallness intrigued him. It would be so easy to toss her against those goose-down-stuffed pillows, open her up and let her ankles dig into his shoulders while he drove in hard.

The easiest and hardest thing in the world.

The image of her perfect breasts arching up to meet

his hungry mouth redirected a wave of blood to his cock. Before she could notice his hard-on, he strode into the bathroom, seeking out two smaller drinking glasses to finish the task at hand. *Focus.*

"You've got me all curious with this fancy-schmancy prep," Neve announced as he came back.

"Nothing but the best for you."

She mashed her lips, gaze riveted to his face. "Who are you and what happened to Tor Gunnar?"

"What do you mean?"

"If I looked up *charming* in the dictionary right now, your face might be staring back. I'm getting a glimmer of Rovhal30 with the daily jokes. Which were corny as a Kansas farmer, by the way." A beat. "And I meant that as a compliment."

He dropped his chin and poured the ginger ale into the vodka, trying not to fizz everywhere. Even though he had a hundred reasons not to smile, she gave him one.

When he placed the smaller glasses on top of the large tumblers, Neve gasped.

"Poor man's cocktail shaker," he confirmed. "Necessity is the mother of invention. And I'm on the road enough that I had to get creative."

"You must miss it, right?" she asked as he mixed their drinks. "Your job? The games? The players? That road? The last two weeks must have felt strange. To put so much buildup and preparation in for a season, get started and . . . poof."

"I miss it every second of every day," he admitted, but

didn't let on the whole truth. He loved his job. He made no apologies for the fact that his work was his life. His passion. But whereas the lockout should be an exercise in torture, it hadn't been as bad as he'd expected. He'd had a distraction. *Her.* "Try this." He cleared his throat and passed her the glass.

"Yup. This'll do nicely—delicious," she said after a small sip, kicking off her snow boots to reveal a pair of brightly colored socks.

Socks that were . . .

"Yeah baby, feast your eyes." She noticed his gawking and smirked. "Rainbow-shitting unicorns."

"On your feet," he deadpanned.

"Socks are one of my weaknesses." She clicked her heels. "These happen to be my favorite pair."

He took a long swallow of his own drink, shoulders dropping. "I don't know what to say about that."

She stared down at her feet, turning them left and right. "We are all allowed to have a vice. Quirky socks are mine."

They cheers'd to that.

"What's your guilty pleasure?" she asked in a mock-conspiratorial tone.

"Dark-haired journalists who bust my balls."

"Hah, I wouldn't quit your day job for stand-up comedy just yet," Neve said after a short silence. After another sip, she set her glass on the nightstand, drew back the comforter and burrowed underneath. "Oy. What a day."

He tensed. "What are you doing?"

"What's it look like I'm doing? It's nap o'clock. You're . . . uh, well . . . welcome to join the party if you don't mind dimming the light."

Tor crossed the room and tugged the blinds back shut. The world disappeared and he was alone in an alternate universe comprised solely of a big bed and Neve Angel.

Chapter Eleven

A COOL LICK of air brushed Neve's cheek as she stirred awake. The floor creaked and creaked again as if someone stealthily tiptoed across the old floorboards. But it couldn't be Tor because he was here. Right here. A shiver ran up her spine before she slit one eye open. Her goose bumps were caused less from unease and more from something warm and molten.

Cheese and rice, how long had she been getting her cuddle on with Tor Gunnar? He was sprawled on his back, his face more relaxed than she'd ever seen in waking. In sleep, her own hand had found its way to his chest and currently rested over his heart, her head nestled in the crook of his shoulder. His blond spikes were mussed on top. And there was the matter of the tiny mole dotting the left side of his bottom lip.

She'd never noticed that mark, had never trusted

herself to stare long enough to register all the little details in his face. To do so would be like staring straight
into the sun. Even now, if she closed her eyes, this image,
his face in repose, was probably seared on her retinas for
all time.

"I'm not drooling, am I?" he rumbled. Not opening
an eye.

"No. No." She moved to draw back her hand and
crawl to safer territory on her side of the giant bed. At
the very least she should apologize for being all over
him like a human barnacle.

Instead, he took her wrist and stopped her retreat,
then slid his hand down until their fingers laced.

They were quiet, in bed and holding hands as if it
were the most natural thing in the world, as if beyond
the drawn curtains a world didn't exist that was black-
and-white, where he wasn't a head coach and she wasn't
the tough-as-nails reporter.

"You're an octopus when you sleep," he murmured.
"An octopus genetically mutated with a honey badger."

"It's a bad habit." Her nose wrinkled in embarrassment. "Breezy used to hate sharing a bed with me when
we were younger. It's annoying."

"Not to me." His Adam's apple rose in a heavy bob.

She lay on her hip, her thigh casually slung over his
waist. The evidence of just how much he didn't mind her
unexpected cuddling bored into her inner thigh.

His body went rigid as if he registered the hard-on at
the exact same moment that she did.

"Neve." He cleared his throat. "I don't want to make this weird."

"Too late." She dared wriggle a fraction closer. "Don't tell anyone but . . . I think we're mutually weird."

"Speak for yourself." He squeezed her hand and finally opened one eye. His pupil was large and dilated in the room's shadows. "You talk in your sleep."

"Sometimes." Her cheeks heated. "I didn't say anything terrible, did I?"

"My name."

Shit a brick. She could never remember her dreams. Hopefully, she didn't tack on anything dirty.

"But then you said, 'Hold the pickles.' So I don't know how to take that."

"Pickles?" Her mouth twitched. "Maybe you were making me another sandwich."

A chuckle rumbled deep in the back of his throat. "Flattering."

"Hey, it was a pretty darn good sandwich."

He opened his other eye, and the force of his stare was seismic. Something shook her deep inside, setting off a core chain reaction that left her flushed and aching.

He mashed his lips before speaking. "I've been meaning to clear the air. I shouldn't have kissed you in the bathroom the other day at The Watering Hole."

She blinked as his words registered, her stomach flipping over. Her free hand slid to the edge of the comforter as the urge swept through her to duck and take cover. Here she was, so lost in this helpless wanting, her sensitive underbelly on full display. And he was about to let her down, remind her that she didn't tempt him, that she never could—

"Because I'd been thinking about that kiss for a hell of a long time and it might have deserved a more up-scale location."

She swiped her top lip with the tip of her tongue. "Well, you didn't hear it from me, but kissing burns six calories a minute. And I didn't get any exercise on the car ride."

His gaze darkened, tracing the shape of her mouth with such intense heat that it was a surprise her skin didn't respond with a sizzling hiss. "The thing is, see, my thoughts never ended with just one kiss. I kept going. Tasting you . . . everywhere."

Her nipples strained against her bra, volunteering as tribute. "All right, Mr. Big Talk. Are you going to show me or am I going to have to go home and lie in my diary?"

"That all depends," he rumbled.

"On?" She was afraid to move, to breathe, to jinx the magic.

"Whether you want me to."

Her core clenched.

"I want my mouth on every inch of that gorgeous body. But if I do that, I'm taking my time, doing it right until you scream my name. But I won't lift a finger unless you beg."

"A finger?" She pretended to think it over, like the scrap of lace masquerading as panties beneath her jeans hadn't melted into a puddle. "If I'm going to be brought to my knees, I'll expect more than one finger, just FYI."

For a guy who had a reputation for being so cool, he had a heck of a smolder. "I can see about that." She didn't see him move, yet he was closer.

"Go on." Closer still. His sexy-as-sin smile left her salivating. "Ask nicely."

"No." She leaned in and bit the corner of his lower lip. "Nothing about this is going to be nice."

When they came together, it was like there'd never been any distance to close, like they'd never done anything else in their lives. Her mouth felt as if it had been made just for him. His lips fit against hers perfectly. When he coaxed, she opened and his tongue slid against hers, the heat of the kiss surging to the tips of her toes. She put her whole body into the answer. Her arms wrapped around his neck, his muscles bunching and cording beneath her fingers. He grabbed her hips and rolled her on top. The hard length of his cock drilled into her lower belly as he grabbed her ass and pressed her down hard.

This wasn't soft.

This wasn't romantic.

It was clawing. Savage. And fucking amazing.

His fingers worked their way up to the waist of her jeans and, dipping under, he paused.

"This is interesting." His light snap of her panties' elastic waistband made her gasp.

"And very tiny," she teased.

His swallow was audible.

His hands migrated to her front, and with a quick button pop and zipper grind, her jeans came down. She kicked them off her ankles.

"Sit up. I want to see you." His voice was deeper and rougher than she'd ever heard.

"Has anyone ever said that you are bossy?"

"Mostly you. I think you like it though." He brushed his thumb along the seam of her pussy, encased in the pale pink silk, scorching her with his possessive gaze. "Not going to lie, it seems as if you like it. A lot."

She was so wet that the material skimmed over her, his touch the lightest whisper of pressure against her clit. Her hands balled into fists and her head rocked back.

"Good?"

"Not bad," she gasped.

"Still sassy." He eased one finger inside her underwear, and inside her.

Good lord, she could hear it, the soft sucking sound of her own arousal. Her muscles tensed in expectation.

"You wanted more than a finger, right?" He joined it with another. That was good. Perfect, really. Enough that she felt full without being too stretched. His eyes glittered.

"Yes," she gasped.

"Fuck, Neve." He trembled. She felt it right there, at the core of herself, at the center of everything. He crooked the fingers up in a come-hither gesture and her body bowed.

"Take off your shirt," he crooned.

She raised her brows, even as her hips began to rock as if of their own volition. "You first."

"Now who's bossy?"

"The way I see it, two can play at this game."

"Fair enough." He had to pull his hand free. She hadn't thought it through, because that was the last thing she wanted.

He raised those fingers that had just been buried inside her to his mouth and slid them inside. "You taste better than I imagined," he rumbled. "And believe me. I imagined."

It was so sexy and filthy that she almost came from his words alone.

But then he unbuttoned his shirt and she forgot everything. How to breathe. Her own name. Sliding her hands down, she parted his shirt to reveal a smooth chest, a light dusting of hair framing each nipple. His chest was broad and his abs weren't individually defined but flat and lean.

She circled his navel. Here it was—definitive proof he was a man, not a god. But good lord, he was beautifully made. She bent and licked the center of his chest, savoring the muscle with the flat of her tongue.

He frowned like thunder, a faint sheen of sweat at his temples. "Keep that up and you'll be in trouble."

"Good." She licked again. "I like your version of trouble."

It wasn't clear who undressed who. Clothes came off in short order. It wasn't until she went to slip out of her pale underwear that he stopped her. "No. Not those. Those I need to enjoy a little while longer. Then I'm going to rip them off with my teeth."

She clenched her inner muscles and dropped her gaze to his boxer briefs, the erection straining the black cotton. "I can't say the feeling is mutual." She wanted him bare, Tor Gunnar in the flesh, and for her pleasure. A tug of the waistband and she had him exposed in all his glorious thick inches.

He was rock hard.

She did that to him.

He sucked in so sharply that his lower ribs stood in sharp relief. In her time working in the Hellions locker room, she'd seen many specimens of the perfect male form, in all their hard, chiseled, athletic glory.

But Tor, he managed to exude brute strength and arrogant confidence just by breathing. And yet stripped down, there was a whisper of vulnerability. Not embarrassment, just a sense that he was offering himself up, exposing more than just his body. He was the definition of a closed book and now here he was, cracking the cover and giving her a peek at who he was beneath.

She wasn't sure what to make of it, but was certain of one fact: Good God, he was perfect. Cut and long. He was rock hard and it was all for her. She didn't feel like an ugly duckling. She didn't even feel like a beautiful swan. The predatory hunger in his wolfish gaze made her feel like a sex kitten, ready to purr, to arch, to drag her claws down his back and mark her territory.

"I love you looking at me like that," he murmured in a low, intense voice.

"Then you're going to adore me after I do this." She moved to lick his shaft but he pushed down on her shoulders, halting her mouth, mere inches away from her desired target.

"Damn it. No," he rasped, even as his eyes were glazed and eager. His chest—sheeted in sweat—rose and fell in uneven breaths.

"You don't want me to?"

"Not yet." His head shake was short but definite. "I want to take my time with *you*. You touch me the way I am right now and it's going to be over too soon. Not going to lie, it's been a while for me."

"Same." She gave a frustrated laugh. "Look at us, arguing over oral."

A flicker of provocative mischief crossed his face as he reached down and lifted her chin, drawing her away. "There is one solution. A win-win."

She gave his gorgeous cock a longing glance. "I'm all ears." A bead of precum gleamed from the tip, refracting light like a diamond.

"How are you at multitasking?"

"I'm a woman." She furrowed her brow, unsure where he was going with this. "It's sort of our specialty."

"Then how about flipping over. I want to lick your sweet pussy while my cock's halfway down your throat."

Whoa.

Of all the things that could happen when Tor's

ice-cold veneer melted, this was more than she'd dared hoped to discover.

He didn't treat her like something fragile or delicate. Far from it. He seemed to know exactly what she wanted—to use and be used in return.

Her thighs pressed together on instinct, the slick caress of her panties almost too much sensation against her mound.

"Go on." He nudged her, his gaze more wicked by the moment. "I promise I'll make it worth your while. You're going to come while I fuck that pretty face."

He knew what he was doing. Oh, this man knew exactly what sort of effect his dominance had on her. She wanted him to take her in every position he could think of. But she paused halfway through her pivot, trying to process what was about to happen.

Intensity and hesitation warred within.

"Neve." His voice seemed to ache with the same need gripping her, squeezing at her center, throbbing through her thighs.

"I . . . I feel sort of shy?" She was acutely aware of just how small her underwear was and the fabric was more or less see-through given her wetness.

"You just tore off my pants."

"Hey. I'm allowed these feelings."

"Right now you're only allowed to be one thing." She felt the force of his gaze like a tantalizing caress.

"Illuminate me." Her voice was faint.

"Hungry for my cock."

Blue stars exploded on the edge of her vision.

That was it. He won all the dirty talk forever. She couldn't beat his mastery, but needed to regain some power. Some foothold here in the bedroom. He wanted to be dominant, that was fine. She was here for it.

But if she was going down, she'd bring him to his knees.

Crawling up, she spread her legs over his face, her knees pressing into his broad shoulders.

She expected him to slide her panties to the side and feast. That was what she'd mentally prepared for. Instead, he stared, stroking the ledge of her panties leg elastic until she was almost begging him for relief. Then slowly, oh, so slowly, he slid a finger under the thin, soaking fabric and hissed a breath.

"Good lord." It sounded like he had to force the words out. "Do you always get this wet?"

Her ears turned pink. The room was so quiet that she could actually hear herself as he stroked her.

"You smell incredible," he growled. "And I already know you taste even better." And then he was there, driving his tongue straight into the center of her slick, tight pussy.

Her mouth opened in a silent scream, and she let her lips close around his shaft. He tasted like clean, warm skin with a faint trace of salt. She circled her tongue around his smooth head and the tangy flavor intensified, as did the shuddering in his muscles.

She'd never done this, never worked over a guy's shaft

while he brought her the same pleasure. She gripped his hard thighs, back arching, as the connection thrummed between them. When she took him down all the way to his root and held him there, pressed against the back of her throat, she relaxed the muscles so she could accommodate his last impressive inch while grinding down on his hungry mouth. True to his word, he fell on her like a starving man and she twisted and turned her hips, grinding over his face with so much greed that she'd be embarrassed if she wasn't so needy.

He groaned and she felt the sensations all the way to her core.

Her heart thundered and then he was there, nipping at her clit, setting a slow, fluttering pace that was gentle and yet increased in pleasure. She bobbed her head, gripping him at the base. He was big enough that it took all her focus to ease him down her throat, and yet she couldn't concentrate. She braced her hands on the mattress, her fingers digging into the sheets.

The sound that came out of her was so bare, so exposed and needy. It was a cry of near want. A mewl. She'd never believed she was able to make such a helpless sound. He hooked three fingers inside her. Crooking his fingers, he pressed hard. She didn't just see stars but the origins of the entire universe and the forever blackness that preceded everything. And she made that sound again and again.

She was coming. The force of it slammed her head down on him, and she felt his legs tense as his cock throbbed. He was there too. And she'd brought him to that point.

He lunged a tongue down straight into her contracting pussy and that decided it. She'd never swallowed. Never wanted to with another guy. But her brain must be blown because she reached down, skimmed his sac with the bottom of her finger and he lost himself.

"Fuck," he groaned. "Fuck. Holy fucking shit."

She took it all, loving every second. Shudders racked them. Their bewildered cries vibrated into their most secret skin. All she knew for certain was that she had one hell of an unfolding crisis on her hands. Because while Tor Gunnar might be infuriating, he was also completely irresistible.

Chapter Twelve

"SORRY THERE, MR. Pie, I want cake," Neve rambled in a husky voice.

Tor choked down a laugh. Good one. She'd woken him a half hour ago with more sleep talking, most of it unintelligible gibberish, but some lines were pure gold:

Into the dungeon!

Is it shank *or* shark? *Never mind, he had it coming.*

Grey dawn light seeped beneath the curtains. He hadn't moved a single muscle, unwilling to break the strange spell spun around the bed, even to taste her soft lips. This moment was good—better than good. The mattress a perfect balance between soft and hard, her naked body spooning into his. When was the last time he'd felt this relaxed in his own skin, this peaceful—

"You have to die," she announced drowsily, eyes still closed. "But it's okay because it's funny."

Christ. She was something else. His brow wrinkled in amusement as he smoothed a strand of damp hair over her flushed cheek. Maybe not peaceful, but one thing was for certain—being in the company of Neve Angel was anything but dull.

Memories from the night before engulfed him like a rising river, leaving him tossed about and breathless. The lithe weight of her body settling over his torso. The shy way she initially ground into his mouth, tentative at first but more confident and insistent as the need set in. Never had he experienced anything close to the wild urgency that had taken hold. It wasn't as if he'd spent the past twenty years as a meat-and-potatoes missionary man, but he'd never been that uninhibited. The idea of loosening up was as foreign as another language. It was hard to take down walls that he'd built during his earliest childhood.

For the first thirteen years of his life, he'd watched his father systematically abuse his mother. There'd been the time when he was seven and jumped in front of his mom, facing down his drunken father with a scream of rage. *Stop hurting her!* Dad didn't listen. That time he hurt Tor too, took him into the garage and beat welts into his ass with jumper cables. Afterward, his mom made him put his hand on the family Bible and promise to never speak up when his dad drank again, to stay quiet and never *ever* air their family's dirty laundry in public. Not to relatives. Not to teachers. The worst thing a person could do was share their business. And then she got the cancer and his old man quit drinking and took up religion, never losing an opportunity to praise his dead wife as the best woman he'd ever known.

Tor frowned darkly. He couldn't find a way to forgive or forget. Dad had ruined his mother's life as a lousy husband. A waterfall of crocodile tears couldn't bring her back. In college the next year, on a hockey scholarship, Tor had declared a major in psychology. He'd never felt easy with other people, and yet, it seemed smart to get a better understanding of the way they ticked. What motivated them. What enraged them. Their hopes. Their dreams.

And he was damn good at the subject, at least when it came to his specialty—sports psychology. But when it came to women, all bets were off. He didn't understand them. But he also knew why. He was afraid to get close to them. He'd lived through his parents' devastated marriage and then his own. He'd learned his lessons from childhood well, too well—suck it up, don't cry, don't feel—and despite every wish to the contrary, had never been able to fully drop his guard. Even with Maddy. Instead, he put his head down, toiled like a caveman hunting water buffalo. And it worked. He had professional success. No one could fault him as a good provider.

But it hadn't been enough. Apparently the old saying was true and money couldn't buy happiness.

Thump.

The noise came from the bathroom.

"Enchilada," Neve mumbled.

The Adeline was an old hotel. It could have been a pipe—hot water kicking on in another room.

Just as he began to turn, ready to wake Neve up with that certain ear-sucking trick that drove her wild last night— *Slam!* The bathroom door banged shut.

He jerked. "What the hell?" He swung his legs out from under the blanket. Feet pounding the floor, he grabbed a towel and slung it around his bare waist. "Olive, honey? Is that you?"

Silence answered.

He walked around the corner. No one was there. He opened the bathroom door and flicked on the light. His own reflection stared back. A bite mark on his chest.

No one was there.

Goose bumps broke out across the base of his neck as he turned to check the windows. All were closed.

"Mmm, what's going on?"

Tor turned around as Neve rubbed two fists, grinding the sleep from her eyes.

"Nothing," he said quickly. Not wanting to look like a Ghostbuster. "Nothing at all. Just checking the weather." He opened the curtains. The peaks were shrouded in iron-grey clouds. A few sullen flakes swirled past the window, hit the small balcony and disappeared. "Might snow later."

"I'm not that big of a cold-weather fan." Her gaze focused on his chest. "I prefer it warmer. Hot even."

It was cute how she checked him out. Her cheeks were a little flushed and her hair looked freshly fucked.

They hadn't gone that far and yet . . . he had the unsettling sensation of seeing her more exposed than she'd been last night, writhing and falling apart over his hungry mouth.

"Have I grown horns?" She patted the top of her head in a self-conscious gesture.

"No." He picked up his dead cell phone and plugged it into the charger.

"That's it," she asked with mock incredulity. "That's the sum total of your reaction? And here I gave you a perfect setup for a *horny* joke. Most guys would have gone for it."

"I'm not most guys."

She nodded. "Ain't that the truth." But she didn't sound like she poked fun. No, she sounded as confused as he felt. "Tor," she said, right as he said, "Neve."

"Ladies first."

"Last night . . ." She hiked the sheets against her chest, hiding the swell of her breasts. "I—look—do we need to talk about what happened last night?"

"You don't sound like you want to?" He was expecting a conversation, to make a game plan to set some ground rules. Neve was the bravest, strongest woman he knew. She faced down his bullshit and called him on it every time. And here she was, wiggling into her lace bra and tiny panties and sliding past him as if she hadn't swallowed him balls deep. As if they were strangers.

"I don't know what to think, let alone what to say. Honestly, I'd rather get up, take a shower and go for a run."

The room was haunted all right, by all the things going unsaid. He had two choices. Start rebuilding his walls or build a bridge to Neve.

"Want company or is this a solo mission?"

She gave him a double take. "Are you asking to share my shower?"

"The forecast is for a lighter-than-normal snowfall in the Rockies this winter. I figured I'd be proactive with water conservation."

"Is that a fact?"

"Hey. No pressure. But if you're on the fence, I'm an excellent back washer." He kept his tone light even against the weight of her assessing stare. He was putting himself so far out there that the branch he was clinging to might crack and fall at any second.

"Okay," she relented and it was all he could do not to exhale. "But I like a hot shower."

"I like anything that involves steam and you being naked," he said gravely.

She did a double take again and burst out laughing. "I never knew you were funny. I like it."

"I'm being serious." He winked. "Come on, Angel. I'll scrub your back and then you can scrub mine."

The tub was an old claw-foot. They were already barely dressed, so it was short work to drop the towels and step into the warm spray once it hit the proper temperature.

"Fancy meeting you here," Neve said, tilting her head back, eyes closing as the water streamed through her dark hair. He took the opportunity to look his fill. Her areolas were small, the size of a quarter, and pale pink, like the inside of a conch shell. They rose up, puffing out from the smooth mound of each breast, as if little invitations. His mouth watered but he forced self-control, even as his cock heated, rising proud and resistant.

Her hips were narrow, the bones in each one sharp and hard. But her stomach was soft, the faintest hint of a belly, and it fascinated him. He wanted to drop to his knees and kiss her there, then travel lower, settle between her open thighs and lick her past the point of sanity.

"I know you're staring." She wiped her eyes and glanced down.

"I want you." He spoke plainly, the need for her, to possess her, to make her his if only for a few stolen moments, left him without the ability to tease, flirt and banter. "But I'll have to go to the store and grab condoms if we're going to go further."

"Did you fail Eagle Scouts?" Her gaze shot to his face. "I thought, like, every guy kept one in his wallet."

"I don't do the whole hookup thing," he admitted. "I haven't been with a woman in a long time."

"*Long* sounds different depending on the person. I knew a guy who considered it a drought if he went longer than two weeks. And I can tell you right now that my dry spell is years. Literally years."

"Same. Seven to be exact."

That got her attention. "Seven years?"

"Since my divorce. I . . . haven't been with another woman like that. Or at all."

"Same. Not the part about being with another woman. I mean seven years. That's where I'm at."

Now it was his turn to be surprised. "But you're so . . . sexy."

"I could say that same for you." She reached out and rested a hand over his heart. "But I am on the pill, have been since sixteen. If you're serious about this whole dry-spell thing, we could, you know . . ."

"You're sure?"

"Let me process." She pressed her hands over her eye. "I'm considering having sex with Tor Gunnar. It's a lot to take in."

"I hear he's a great lay. And did I mention the charm?"

She dropped her arms to her sides. "If I have one nemesis in this world, it would be you, Mr. Fuck-a-Penguin. But maybe the altitude's getting to me. Because the idea of you inside me is . . ." She broke off, searching for the precise word.

"Nice?"

She made a face. "Puppies are nice. So is chocolate milk. Sex with you would be the reverse of nice." She peered up, nibbling the corner of her lower lip. "Bad in the best of ways."

"We're doing this. You want it?"

"I think . . . yes. I am amenable to having your penis inserted into my vagina."

"Inserted?"

"Injected? Implanted."

Nothing about her jokingly clinical tone should make him hard, and yet . . . his cock twitched. "Maybe leave the dirty talk to me, babe."

"So how do we start?" Neve's uncertain laugh echoed from the tiles. "It feels like I'm Cinderella getting an erotic offer to the ball."

"I recommend we do a little of this." He closed the distance, then wrapped his arms around her hot, slippery body. His mouth found hers and there was nothing in this kiss but confidence.

For all he didn't know about women—particularly the woman in his arms—he knew he wanted this. And maybe once he was inside her, everything would make sense.

Even though he held her tight, making sure she was completely kissed, her head tilted back as his tongue boldly explored hers. She remained curious. Her hands exploratory and restless. She roamed his lats, grabbing and squeezing as if trying to root out softness. A wild hope flared that maybe he'd finally found a woman he could open up to and risk exposing his secret sensitive underbelly. A woman who was fearless. Who wouldn't run from his demons. Who wouldn't flinch or back down if she saw him for who he was.

"Hurry," she pleaded. "I need—"

"I know exactly what you need," he growled. And the thing was, he did.

He hadn't touched a woman in years. And yet . . . he knew how Neve was going to want him. Not slow and gentle this first time. He flipped her around. "Stick out that sweet ass for me, Angel."

Her gasp was audible but she obliged. He bent and licked and bit the side of her neck until she rocked against him.

Sliding down a hand over her trembling belly, he cupped her pussy, held it in a firm grasp. "This is mine."

She leaned back, her hands pushing off the tile. "If you can earn it."

"Challenge accepted." He wasn't going to pop in a finger or two and rub until it was wet enough for his dick. This was a focused, deliberate campaign. He wasn't going to stop until she'd fallen apart, her smart talk replaced by begging. And that would only be the beginning. He put his dominant hand over her clit, already beginning to swell like a hot pearl. With his left, he slipped a finger inside, just the tip, caressing her inner lips with slow, gentle pumps.

"Do you like it better when I fuck you with two fingers or three?" he murmured in her ear.

"The more the merrier . . ." she panted.

"Greedy." He obliged and she arched, the crease in her ass sliding over his cock, working his shaft in a tight clench.

His fingers were soon covered in her natural lube. He got the best reaction when keeping the pressure right on the rough patch a few inches into her pussy. When he pressed the top of her pubic bone with the heel of his hand, it became more exposed.

"Oh God, oh my God," she groaned. Shudders rolled through her with growing intensity.

He switched over from the light pressure on her clit, drawing back the hood and giving a few quick taps as he pressed harder to her G-spot.

Her head fell back and he leaned in over one shoulder and kissed her hard, let her scream into his mouth, holding up her weight as she collapsed against him. The force of her orgasm broke over his fingers, milking them in waves.

Her lips parted, her eyes glazed. "I've never come that hard in my life."

"That's going to be a short-lived record." He spun her around, grabbed one of her legs and propped it on the edge of the tub.

If he wasn't in her in another second, he'd lose his damn mind.

"Look down," he ordered. "I want you to watch me take you. There's going to be no doubt who's making you feel so good."

"Tor . . ."

"That's right." He pressed the head of his cock against her. "When you're screaming again, it's going to be my name."

"Okay."

"Promise?"

"Pinky promise. I'll watch. I'll scream. But . . . will you?" Her eyes dared him.

It was a tight fit. She was still clenched from her recent orgasm and he wasn't a small guy. He took his time, rocking his hips in short micropulses.

And she was a woman of her word. What he didn't expect was how watching her slowly become undone would slay him.

"You're so beautiful," he said.

Her eyes shone. "You're the first person to make me believe it."

He tilted up her chin—what he had to say was important and she needed to hear that truth to the marrow of her bones. "This confirms my long-held suspicion." His tone was grave. "The world is mostly made up of idiots." He leaned in and kissed the tip of her nose. "But all the better for me."

He began to move, dissolving into her skin, his hands memorizing the topography of her body as if to mark the path—he was lost. Lost in her. In this slow, sucking grind. The slap of their bellies wasn't subtle. It was the bass note to the song they were writing. Her soft cries, the chorus.

It was hard to keep the rhythm steady. The control he had cared about was gone. He wasn't going to dominate her. The idea was a joke. Because the truth was he could never possess her without losing a part of himself. And he was willing to make the devil's bargain.

His finger dug into the underside of her thigh. He

gripped her roughly, trying to keep them balanced while getting them both where they needed to go.

His whole world was wet heat. The shower spray. Neve's pussy. His stomach flexed as the need bore down. He'd never forgotten how good it felt to be in a woman. Maybe that was why he'd resisted for so long. It was his punishment for failing in his marriage.

But Neve already knew he wasn't perfect. Hell. She'd seen him surly and snappish. Cold and calculating. And for some unfathomable reason, she was still here. Maybe she'd hate him again tomorrow. But he sure as hell wasn't ever going to let her regret today.

And close as he was—his sac heavy and tight—he wasn't coming without her. He stepped back. Nearly groaning when his cock slipped free. Before she could ask him a word, he flicked off the shower.

"Come here," he ordered, stepping out of the tub. He grabbed a large plush bath towel, threw it open and sat on the floor. "Get on top."

She looked at him, sex dazed and pleasure drunk. When she crawled onto him, draping her thighs on either side of his, he fastened his lips to her throat as she slid down, enveloping him. "Ride me rough, Angel."

Her sex clenched as her eyes glittered. No tears this time. Just hot determination.

Tor rubbed slow circles into her perfect ass as she worked her body, using him while giving everything he ever needed.

He cupped her breasts, rolling and tugging her

nipples. Steam filled the room from the hot shower, the condensation comingling with their sex. His lower back arched, tilting his pelvis so she could grind her tender flesh right where she needed. A tremor rippled through her, invisible to the outside but stroking his shaft.

He leaned up and sucked her tit, lavishing it with his tongue and gentle nips. He felt her groan in his core, at his goddamn center. He was primed as fuck but wasn't giving an inch until her surrender. Hunger built. Release taunted. Blood roared through his ears. Her teeth closed down on her lower lip as if biting back a scream.

He gripped her hips, white-knuckled. Her ass bounced on his thighs.

"I need," she gasped. "I need . . . I need . . ." She shook her head as if to clear it. "I just *need.*"

"I know, Angel." He breathed as hard as she did. "I know."

Her gaze never left his. An undefinable sense of rightness bore down. They were at the edge of a precipice.

When her pussy spasmed, he muffled a groan. She thrashed, bucking, riding him harder than cowboys in the spaghetti Westerns he'd watch as a child. Her thighs convulsed. His abs tightened.

This need for her was a drug. Heady and obsessive. Intoxicating.

She was close. So close. A strand in his threadbare self-control snapped.

"Come," he ordered. His tone hard with the command. "Come for me."

Her hands flew up and dug into his hair.

He quickened the roll of his hips. "Let go. I've got you."

Her whole body jerked. With a throaty gasp, she froze into place, the stillness deceptive because inside she was clenching, her orgasm rolling over his cock from root to tip in an undulating, silken wave.

And then he was there too. Pleasure exploded from him in thick, hot pulses. On and on it went, wringing him dry, demanding nothing less than complete surrender. How many times had they warred with each other? And at last they'd found a battle they could both win.

She fell against him, utterly sated.

He didn't ask her how it was, because he already knew. That was just the single most goddamn explosive sexual event west of the Mississippi. He rubbed slow circles into her back and time turned abstract. At last he nudged her. "Hey."

"Hi." She looked over at him with a sleepy smile.

"How about I draw you a bath, get you cleaned up?" He smoothed back her hair.

She gave a dazed nod.

He moved into action and it didn't take long until the claw-foot tub brimmed with hot water and lemongrass-scented bubbles. After picking her up and cradling her in his arms, he lowered her into the tub. She let out a soft hiss as the warm water enveloped her body.

"I don't feel like I have a bone in my body." Her eyes remained closed.

He picked up a washcloth and dipped it into the

bath, soaking it. Moving it over her body, he cleaned her with gentle caresses. No words were spoken. It wasn't that he didn't know what to say but that words simply didn't matter. All that did was this simple act of caring. With every touch, he worshipped her body and what had just transpired.

"I need to be honest about something," he murmured.

Her eyelids cracked. "You've got my attention."

"When I invited you to come to Telluride, deep down, I wanted this to happen." He took a deep breath. "I wanted us to happen. I know it's risky for you. For me. But I wanted a weekend. Just one to remember."

A frown tugged her pretty mouth. "You've never been straight with me about something." She sat up, bubbles clinging to her breasts, covering her nipples. "The night the lockout was announced. Why did you say all those terrible things in the parking lot?"

The pain in her eyes twisted his gut.

"Because the world doesn't get to know the secrets of my heart." He reached out to take her hand and give it a gentle squeeze. "But that night was a mistake. I panicked and lashed out. When I saw the other reporters, I didn't want them to think something was going on. That wouldn't be good for either of us."

"Not going to lie. It sucked. But you're right about one thing. There's a lot of risk here. I cover your team. I can't exactly *be* with you and pretend to be fair and balanced."

He pushed back a lock of hair from her cheek. "You could cover football. The NFL has a lot going for it."

"That better be a joke."

"I see, you prefer ice sports. What about curling?" He tickled behind her ear. "That's cool."

"You have some sort of a death wish, huh, wise guy?"

He sucked the lobe of her ear just long enough to make her gasp. "Just wanted to see that pretty smile again."

But her answering grin didn't reach all the way to her eyes. "My kind of job doesn't just spring into being. I had to bust my ass to get where I am. Sports journalism isn't a field rolling out the red carpet for a woman. Being here, with you, having, you know . . . *sex*? That's complicated. I'm not saying I didn't enjoy it. I'm not saying that."

"Why did you come? I know it wasn't for the bet, at least not alone. You could have found an excuse."

"I'm curious. I guess I—"

A phone rang in the other room.

Chapter Thirteen

WHAT THE HECK does Scott Miller want? Neve glanced at her phone. Her pain-in-the-butt editor had called three times in as many minutes, disrupting her bath. She took a deep breath. *Look on the bright side.* While annoying, maybe this call was the adult version of getting saved by the bell. She'd had her fantasy fun—time to get a taste of reality.

She stared at the screen, debating whether or not to hit Answer. Hard to switch gears when she'd just spent the past twelve hours getting up close and personal with the head coach's baby maker. Right now he was in the bathroom brushing his teeth. She could hear the scrub of bristles against his enamel. A spit. The sound of the faucet turning on as he rinsed his mouth.

She flicked off the screen and ran her fingers through her hair.

How was this happening?

She understood the concept of hate fucking. After all, love and hate were opposites, so a certain magnetic attraction made sense given the right circumstances. And Tor was sexy. It was an objective fact. Like the sky was blue. Or sucking hard candies was pretty much drinking flavored spit.

What she had done with Tor could be called many different things.

Passionate.

Tender.

Sweet.

IntensemindblowingcanIlockthehotelroomdoorandspendthenexttwodaysdoingitanddoingitanddoingitwell?

But it wasn't hate sex. It wasn't quick and dirty in some broom closet in the bowels of the stadium. She'd gone on vacation with him. There could be no slinking away into the shadows thinking, *Good lord, that was incredible, and not only can it never happen again, no one can know.*

Who knew what Scott was calling about, but she'd call him back downstairs, outside, before they went on the valley run.

Speaking of a run, she slipped on her tennis shoes, laced them up as Tor came out of the bathroom.

His running pants clung to his hard muscles like a second skin. His quads rose, thick and defined, while his hips were tapered. Abs flat. The merest suggestion of a bulge, if someone wanted to get their perv on.

Which, God help her, she did.

"Like what you see?" He gave her a wry look.

"I . . . just had something in my eye. Dust." She rubbed her lids in an unconvincing pantomime. She wasn't going to be winning acting awards for her "lady doth protest too much" routine.

"Dust. Is that what they are calling getting hot under the collar?"

"Hot under the collar? I think my granny Dee uses that expression."

"Your granny Dee sounds like she has a way with words."

She grinned. "My granny is also ninety."

His mouth twitched. "I've been meaning to ask. How old are you?"

"I thought that question is off-limits once a lady passes the age of twenty-nine."

Something like relief settled over his features. "So you are over thirty."

"Fine," she huffed. "I *am* thirty. Turned June 2nd. Gemini." She threw out her hands in a ta-da gesture.

"I'm forty."

"Congratulations?" She raised her brows. "Given the circumstances, it's fair to say we are both of a certain age. Like in cavemen times, at thirty I'd be ready to call it a life after having sixteen kids and once eating a handful of berries, so have some perspective. It's not like I'm fourteen and you're twenty-four. Speaking of which, the year I was fourteen, that was a good time. The iPhone came out. The craziest news was that Brittany Spears shaved her head."

"Simpler days."

"No doubt." She bent into a deep leg stretch, preparing for the upcoming run. "I'm more grizzled and the world harsher. And you sure as heck aren't going to be able to do much to corrupt me and/or my delicate virtue at this point."

He inclined his head. "Bet I *can* kick your ass in a sprint."

"Oh, you didn't go there."

He made a show of glancing around. "Pretty damn sure I just did."

And while what had happened with him in the bed, in the tub and, God help her, on the bathroom floor over the past few hours gripped her in uncertainty, on this point there would be no doubt: Tor Gunnar would eat her dust. She'd outrun her confusion and hopefully, at the end she'd arrive at clarity.

When they walked out of the room, an Adeline staff member moved to the side, pushing a room service cart down the hall. He gave a friendly smile before glancing at the room number.

"Room 309, huh? How'd you sleep?" He said the room number like it meant something.

Neve furrowed her brow as her stomach muscles tensed. How loud had they just been? Good lord, had the people around them complained? If so, she was ready to get a shovel and bury herself inside the nearest snowdrift. "I'm not sure," she said hesitantly as the guy was clearly expecting an answer and not making idle chitchat.

"That's good. Lots of the maids won't even clean in there. They have to draw straws."

"Why?" Tor asked in his usual no-nonsense tone. Even casually dressed for a run he had a way of looking in charge, aloof and cool—a master of the universe. Nothing like the guy who fell apart against her last night, a helpless look in his normally ice-blue eyes. Her mouth dried as she remembered his raw growl as he came undone in her mouth.

If she didn't have a stubble burn on her inner thighs, she'd almost be inclined to believe it was all a dream. The sexiest dream she'd ever had, but impossible to conceive.

"They didn't tell you at check-in?" The staffer seemed honestly surprised. "It's often specifically requested by guests, as a test."

"Test of what?" Tor asked, clearly inching toward impatience. His jaw was beginning to tighten and his gaze narrowed.

"The dueling ghosts can predict your love. Adeline Rose and Big Jim Cartwright."

She and Tor exchanged quick glances.

"I'm sorry, can you please elaborate on this?" she asked. "I can't say I'm familiar with dueling ghosts or love predictions."

"There's a plaque about it downstairs next to the

front desk, but they say they only make an appearance if a couple is the real deal, so congrats! Now I've got to deliver these eggs to the bride before they get cold. There's going to be a wedding tonight." He whistled as he wheeled the breakfast cart away up the hall.

"I was bound and determined to get coffee before anything else, but I sort of think we have to go see this plaque." She peered closer. "You look pale. What gives? Did you see Slimer floating around last night? Or maybe a giant Stay Puft marshmallow man wandering by the window?"

"No . . . but . . ." He shook his head as if to clear it. "Never mind."

"Are you sure?" A chill stole down her spine. "For real, you're starting to scare me a little."

"Let's go take a look at the plaque." His tone was impassive. "Then we run."

Down in the lobby, right near the check-in desk was a silver plaque beside a turn-of-the-century black-and-white wedding photo where neither half of the stern-faced couple appeared remotely happy.

"Why are people always so serious-looking in these old-timey photos?" she murmured.

"They had to hold still for so long. Forcing a smile might have been too hard."

She pointed at the plaque and began reciting the text. "'Adeline Rose and Big Jim were a famous bank-robbing duo known for their passionate arguments and even more passionate makeups. After a bank heist in

Grand Junction, they came to Telluride to hole up at Adeline's sister's brothel. But for reasons no one is entirely clear on, the feisty couple got into an argument in their room. The result was a duel in the street out in front of the brothel. They walked ten paces and each turned to fire. Neither aimed to miss.' And get a load of this last part." Neve nudged Tor. "'But the two deadly lovebirds seemed to have found peace in the afterlife. Couples in love often find ghostly signs from the duo and take it as a sign of good luck.' I guess that's one way to spin a sketchy situation. Kudos to The Adeline's marketing team."

"You aren't armed and dangerous, are you?" Tor murmured in her ear, his breath heating her skin.

"If anyone is packing a big weapon here, it's you." She turned and glanced between his legs with an arch look.

His laugh was short and gruff. "Your sexual-innuendo game is as strong as your sarcasm."

She smirked. "And here I didn't even know that I possessed this rare talent until spending time in your orbit."

His frank gaze went wolfish. "I can't stop wondering what other rare talents you possess."

She had the grace to blush even as heat sparked between her legs. "I suppose you got a taste last night?"

"And here I am hungry for more."

"You make me sound like your personal smorgasbord."

"Must be the Swede in me," he deadpanned before adding, "But look. Today we're in Telluride together and on a truce. I'd like to spend time hanging out. And maybe with Olive."

"Your daughter." Before she could let the full impact of his invitation sink in, her stupid phone rang. Again. Scott.

"Ugh, I'm sorry. This is my boss. I have to take this. He is being relentless."

"He's being a bastard. But I get it. Work's important. Go ahead and do what you need to do." He paused before turning away. "Oh, and try to resist checking me out while I walk over here to stretch."

That sense of humor, where had he been hiding it?

"Scott. You're persistent." She flicked on her phone, walked across the street and leaned against a streetlight. "I was about to call you back."

"Tell me more, Angel," he snapped. Typical. Her boss always cut right to the chase. Not unlike the man doing calf stretches next to the building across the street. Or at least his old version.

"I don't know what you are talking about."

"Don't play coy. I'm looking here at the last article you sent, and in the email you mentioned you were taking a weekend trip out of the city. To go to Telluride. With Tor Gunnar. What's the deal?"

"Well, it is just . . . I lost this bet and I sort of kind of ended up with him here at this wedding in Telluride."

"Bullshit."

"No bulls. I speak the truth."

No one had a laugh like Scott—a cross between a braying donkey and a hyena.

She'd hear that laugh after the punch line to off-color jokes in the newsroom. Usually referencing women.

Hey, Neve. Why do women make better soldiers? Because they can bleed for a week and not die.

She'd try to eye roll it off. After all, he was happily married. He had a kid up at the University of Wyoming and a grown daughter in Boise. He didn't have groping hands or a wandering, lecherous gaze.

It wasn't like she had some big case to take to Human Resources. What was she going to say? His jokes made her feel annoyed and uncomfortable? That he made her dream job far less dreamy? That he'd been bemused to come into the editor role and find her covering the hockey beat? Once he'd caught wind about her being a former figure skater, it was all over. She'd had to prove she wasn't a girly girl.

What irony—not feminine enough for figure skating but too girly for sports journalism. She wished at this point in history that things like sexism and gender inequality never reared their ugly heads, but the truth was there was a great deal of work still to be done.

When it came to her field, there was an undeniable gender imbalance across print, broadcast and online platforms in sports journalism. Men—especially white men—dominated, while female reporters were left getting nitpicked on the internet about their outfits or bodies rather than respected for their sports punditry.

Sexism sucked and provided yet another reason—besides her lack of a life—to keep her social media interaction to a minimum. If she rocked a good hair day, someone would comment, speculating which player was her current hookup. If she pulled her hair back into a bun or ponytail and looked too severe, she was dismissed as "manly." There was literally no winning. Her boss didn't do too much to add to the culture of toxic masculinity, but he sure as heck didn't do a lot to diminish it.

So she managed.

After all, she'd had experience. Heck, she should add "dealing with the male gaze" under her LinkedIn skill sets.

Finally Scott's laughter dwindled. "So what's the deal. You working undercover on a big story?"

"He knows that I'm a journalist, Scott. More like I'm here as his guest."

"So he invited you?"

"Yes, don't sound so surprised."

"You two aren't an item, right? Because you—"

"No! No. Nothing like that." Those words could be a career killer. How many hockey reporters had ended their careers by getting involved with players or coaches?

Lots.

"Whatever you say. I don't know what you're up to

but I want a story from this, on my desk, first thing Monday. Something juicy."

Yesterday morning she would have given him a thumbs-up and gone in guns blazing. But shifts had happened. Earth-shattering, tectonic fractures.

"I'm not sure that is going to happen."

"What do you mean?" Scott's tone cooled.

"I mean that I don't think I want to be on the record this weekend."

"Sorry." His laugh this time wasn't amused. "Who is Sports editor?"

"Let's not play rhetorical twenty questions. It diminishes both of us."

"Here's what I know. Numbers are down here at the paper. Print is sucking. Digital subscriptions aren't where they need to be. You know what that means?"

"I'm sure you are about to tell me."

"Heads are on the chopping block. And your smart-mouthed head could be added to the pile."

"Is this a threat?" She bristled. "I mean, come on, Scott, we've worked together for a couple years now. You are better than this two-bit 'Mafia gangster meets medieval executioner' routine."

"You think I'm kidding. I'm not. What I'm saying isn't an if. It's a when."

Neve's stomach bottomed out. What she wanted to do was tell her boss to take the bacon cheeseburger that was probably sitting on his desk and cram it down his throat and choke. Not die. She wasn't a monster. But definitely see the light and have a fright. She poured her heart and soul into her career and had always been a team player. Now he wanted to threaten her over reluctance to do some sort of profile on Tor?

But if she refused too hard, he'd get suspicious and he wasn't a subtle guy. The last thing she needed was for it to get around that she'd gone off with Tor for the weekend and send chins wagging. Was she trying to sleep her way into better stories?

God. Men never had to deal with this bullshit.

But she also had a mortgage on her townhome. Her Wagoneer didn't have a payment, but it was old and it wouldn't take long before something big broke down. She couldn't up and move to chase a new job or she'd leave her family. And she didn't want to do that. Denver was home. It was where she belonged.

She had to stick it out, and by hook or by crook she'd do it.

"What's it going to be?" he said.

"Fine." She couldn't risk her job. Not in this current economic climate. She'd have to find a way to sell the idea to Tor. At the very least she'd be up-front about her intentions; she owed him that much.

"Good girl," he said approvingly, then stuck something crunchy into his mouth and chewed away her last nerve.

Good girl.

Like she was an obedient dog. *Sit. Shake. Roll over. Woof. Woof. Woof.* She nearly growled.

"Don't be sulky. I also come bearing good news. Your article on the top-five worst coaches is going great. In the top-five article views and third in most emailed. Nice work."

Oh shit. Her "I come in peace" sales pitch to Tor just took a nosedive. He was never going to believe her when she'd put out that snarky hit piece.

She'd let her petty show and now it had come back to bite her in the butt cheek.

"This is going to be great. You've had a public feud with Gunnar. Now you're down there one-on-one. Pardon my *le Francois* but my instincts are fucking phenomenal. With the lockout in place, we have to keep the masses entertained. This . . . Tor and Neve's Excellent Adventure? It's the gold standard in entertainment."

"Glad to amuse you." She swiveled her head. Tor paced up and down in front of a Western-themed saloon next to The Adeline.

"Don't take this the wrong way, but I never pictured you as Tor Gunnar's type."

"Two things. We're just friends. Well. Sort of for now. And second . . . ouch. Who talks like that?"

"Hey, don't getting sulky on me when I'm just yankin' your chain. But take one look at the guy. He looks like he stepped out of the pages of a Norwegian ad. Looks ready to milk a reindeer or some shit."

"Sweden," she bit off. "His heritage is Swedish."

"You're no fun."

"That goes both ways." She wasn't trying to be cute.

She was a hundred percent serious. "This has been real, but it hasn't been real fun. Listen. I got to go."

"Good luck. I look forward to all the juicy details."

She hung up. "I didn't realize the *Age* had become a tabloid," she snarled under her breath. Shoving the phone into her pocket, she crossed the street. Tension radiated from her muscles. This energy was only going to be expended one way.

Her sex clenched when she met Tor's watchful gaze. Okay, technically there was another way she could expend this tension, but running would leave her with a clearer head. Her boss's words rang in her head. What did a Norse god want with a woman like Neve when he could have anyone?

Ugh. Insecurity was an insidious asshole.

"Think you can keep up, old man?" she called with a wink, feigning an ease she in no way felt.

He took her measure. "Cocky much?"

"Not cocky if it's true. I'm fast."

"You talk more trash than Johnny in 'The Devil Went Down to Georgia.'"

"I guess that makes you the devil." She should tell him about the profile right now. Just blurt it out and be done with it.

"Want to make another wager?"

"Let's do it. I'm feeling lucky." She bit back her tongue to keep from teasing, *And win or lose, I'll probably still get lucky.*

"We get to the river. One mile. Fastest buys the other coffee."

"Sounds good. I look forward to foregoing my usual dark roast. That coffee shop on the corner looks delightful. I'm in the mood for a double-shot mocha. Extra whipped cream. I won't be a cheap date."

"All right. Let's put up or shut up." He gave an "after you" gesture. "Ladies first."

"Why, thank you, good sir."

He grinned and the sun broke through the steely clouds. Yes. She'd ask him about doing the profile. But after the run.

Chapter Fourteen

TOR HAD PLANNED to let her win until halfway through their race. That was when he realized there was no "letting"—he didn't have a prayer. They flew past aspens, their spindly branches bare and ghost white. He pumped his arms, his heavy breaths fogging the wintry air, while she skipped along like frigging Bambi in the meadow for the first time. She looked up and smile lines creased the corners of her eyes.

"Hanging in there? I can dial back the pace if it's too much."

"Fine," he gasped. "I'm fine."

"You sure? Because there's no harm in stopping. It's beautiful, isn't it? We could pull over. Let you rest and catch your breath."

"Angel," he snapped. "You'll be the death of me."

"Stay away from any bright lights." She wiggled her

hips, jogging in place. "I really want to win that coffee. I forgot my wallet."

"What's your average-pace mile?"

"Seven thirty." She didn't even pause before answering. *Jesus.* "That's fast."

She heaved her shoulders in a told-you-so shrug. "I tried warning you."

"You run marathons?"

"Not yet but I'd like to start. You?"

"No."

"Sorry, can you repeat that? It's a little hard to hear you through the panting."

He tried to snort but it came out a wet gasp. "Pace yourself. We're almost at the end. That was a three-quarter-mile mark."

"You're slowing."

He was. By a lot. "Just saving something for the finish."

"Admit defeat. You can't catch me." Her legs pumped faster. "TTFN! See you on the flip side."

He pushed hard, but he couldn't catch her. Once the realization sank in, his frustration was replaced by admiration, and a little ogling of her Lycra-clad ass. He slowed, sucking in greedy gulps of air.

Here was a woman who could kick his ass into next week, and he'd keep coming back for more.

She blew past the mile marker and turned, throwing her arms up like Rocky on the steps of the Philadelphia Museum of Art. Her victory whoop rose into the crisp air, cut off by a thrashing from the undergrowth lining the river.

"Neve!" Tor shouted, lunging forward as a male moose emerged. "Don't move."

A few weeks ago, while lifting at the gym, one of the televisions had showed a feature on dangerous animals. Near the top of the list was the moose, right after the grizzly bear.

Neve's muffled swearing was audible, but the animal blocked any view of her face. The moose stood in the middle of the trail, head raised, ears alert. It was still technically autumn. Had mating season ended? The animal could be merely on the lookout for breakfast or succumbing to raging hormones.

One second went by. Two. Three.

No movement. They were having a moose-off.

"Um . . . Tor?"

The bull grunted at Neve's hesitant call. Its powerful hooves churned gravel on the trail. Deep nostrils flared.

Big Boy didn't look happy. Tor cracked his neck and went into game mode. Shut out panic. Shut out the snow beginning to fall in thicker, heavier flakes. Ignored the physiological sensations currently amping his body, the shortness of breath, tingling limbs, racing heart. He'd coach Neve out of this situation.

"Tor, I'm freaking out. Nature is great and all, but this is too much."

"Listen, Babe. I want you to take a breath. Don't move."

He surveyed the surrounding area. "Do everything I say and you'll be okay."

The moose stamped again. More huffing. Big Boy clocked in at almost seven feet. If he trampled Neve, she'd be in serious trouble—life-threatening trouble.

She whimpered. The moose tossed his shaggy head.

A plan took shape. "Behind you, on the left, is a wooden fence. It's not tall. From there is a forested slope down to the river. On my command, you're going to run as fast as you can, get over that fence and behind a tree."

That way if the moose charged, there would be not one but two barriers to keep her safe while he figured out a distraction.

"You can do this."

"Thanks for the confidence vote, but I don't think I can. My legs are jelly. I might pass out."

"You can and you are. Remember how you whipped my ass in that race?"

No response.

"Neve." That was an order. "Stay with me."

"I just nodded. You just couldn't see it because there's a giant moose blocking the view."

She still had spunk. That counted for something.

He raked fingers through his hair, his hand not quite steady. "Do what I say. I'll take care of the rest. Nothing bad will happen to you. Trust me."

She sniffled. "I do."

The moose kicked out a back leg again. Its long black tongue came out to lick its nose and mouth.

"These things are vegetarian, right?" she asked.

The two bristle-haired ears flattened, the thick hair along the back rising in hackles. Tor didn't need Animal Planet to inform him that this was a clear sign of agitation being replaced by aggression. The moose had two choices, flight or fight. Big Guy appeared to be leaning toward the latter.

"Go," Tor barked sharply. "Go now. Head down, ass in gear."

Neve took off like a shot. He could hear her shoes crunching up the trail.

The moose whirled its big head and Tor picked up a rock, threw it away from the river, away from Neve.

"Hey, you. Pick on someone your own size." Okay, not his finest line, but it didn't matter. The moose didn't speak English. But it did appear to understand a loud, deep voice.

He'd gotten its attention. Neve jumped the fence as the moose turned to face him. No huff this time. This sound was more of a . . . growl.

Shit. Moose growled? There was a fun fact he'd never needed to discover.

As for his lame "pick on someone your own size" comment, the moose rose a foot above him. Not only did the hairy bastard growl, it looked smug about the size difference.

The only choice was to channel the biggest badass he could think of. An image of Samuel L. Jackson from *Snakes on a Plane* came to mind. Good 'nuff.

The moose lunged, as if in a charge. Somewhere from behind the shrubby willows, Neve screamed.

The moose pulled up short. Lifted its great shaggy head and sniffed the air.

A fake out. Well played.

It cocked its head, turning its gaze to him. From end to end, the spread of the animal's antlers must be at least equal to his own height of six-two.

Christ, what did one do with a moose charge? Was it like a grizzly attack, where you were supposed to fall over and play dead? Or was it more of a black-bear situation, where you should fight back?

The moose stamped, the massive slabs of muscles in its chest flexing. Tor frowned. Fuck playing dead. If he fell to the ground and got run over, he'd look like roadkill. Nothing for it but to override his urge for flight and flip the switch to fight mode. Throwing his arms up over his head, Tor faked his own lunge. Arms extended above his head to give the impression that he was larger than he was, he bared his teeth and gave his best snarl.

No reaction.

Shit.

If the moose did charge, those powerful legs were going to hurt. But he had no intention of letting that happen. Tor had a rep for making big gambles that played out. Maneuvers where his players would achieve the impossible, leave fans delighted and opposing teams scratching their heads.

But he'd never physically put himself on the line.

This moose wasn't going to back down without a good reason. He knew a fake out when he saw one.

Time to mean business.

Tor ripped off his running top, grabbed both sleeves and raised it above his head, whipping it wildly. He ran forward screaming. This time he wasn't going to stop. It would be him or the moose. There could only be one. And he knew who would win.

Fifty feet. Forty feet. Thirty feet. The moose held its ground, eyes growing wide.

Tor yelled again. Fifteen feet. Ten feet.

At five feet, the moose veered and ran for the hills. Literally.

Tor bent over, bracing his hands on his knees.

"What the heck were you thinking?" Neve emerged from the woods. "Are you insane? No, don't bother answering. I already know. Yes. Yes, you are. Crazy as they come. You just chased down a frigging moose!"

"I didn't want it to hurt you."

"I've never been so scared, and also turned on." She reached out and touched his abs. "Why did you take your shirt off?"

"I figured it might make me look bigger if I waved it around."

She grabbed him at the elbows. "You. Are. Crazy."

"Come on." He arched a brow. "You aren't a little a-moosed?"

She shook her head even as an unwilling smile tugged her lips. "Too soon."

"It appears I moose-spoke. I moose have thought you had a better sense of humor."

"Tor Gunnar. Head coach. Moose slayer. All-around punny guy."

"It's no joke, make no moose-take."

She groaned, burying her face in his chest.

He kissed the top of her head. "I can keep going."

"I beg you to quit. Seriously, let's get out of here before Bullwinkle on steroids decides to pay a repeat visit."

He slid on his shirt. "Good idea. Plus this snow doesn't look like it's letting up."

They only took a few steps before he noticed she ambled stiffly, like someone trying to repress pain.

"You hurt yourself." Not a question.

"Oh, it's nothing. I just turned my ankle fleeing a giant woodland creature."

"Sprain?" His voice sharp.

"I'm sure it's nothing." But her tone was tight.

"Let's take a look at the nothing." After dropping into a crouch, he moved to roll up her leggings.

She sucked in a sharp breath. "Maybe don't touch. I'll get some ice on it back at the hotel."

"Jesus, you are in pain." It was clear she had swelling. Now standing, he held out his arms. "I'll carry you."

"What? All the way back to the hotel?"

"It's not far."

"A mile!"

"Well, how do I put this? You are little. Are you even five feet?"

She drew herself up to her full small height. "I'm bigger than a penguin, Mister."

He chuckled. "I'm just saying, I think I can manage."

She shifted her weight, hesitating, and winced. "Normally I would rather crawl than ask for help, but my moose fear is overriding my pride."

He scooped her up and cradled her against him. A snowflake landed on the tip of her nose and he kissed it off.

"You've saved me twice before breakfast."

"I'm quite aware of this fact."

"You seem pleased."

"Very much so."

"Smug much?" she asked.

"Always."

They shared a quiet laugh.

"Thank you," she said quietly. "I'm not used to a guy having my back."

"I'd like to have you on your back."

"I'm being serious."

He dropped the teasing. "I know. Truth. I was scared. More than scared back there."

"I couldn't tell."

"If something had happened to you? I don't think I'd have forgiven myself."

"It wasn't your fault. At all. It wasn't even the moose's fault. It probably wanted to catch a quick bite before this snow and we upset its mojo. But . . . I was scared too. Watching you on that trail. I haven't felt like that before."

"I'm hazarding a guess that there've been times in our past you'd have paid good money to hire a moose to pay me a little visit."

She wrinkled her nose. "I'm going to plead the Fifth on that one."

"All right, confession time. Here's the deal. I never disliked *you*, Neve. I hated how you made me feel."

"And how was that?" she murmured.

"Like my heart was trying to climb out of my chest."

"Sounds uncomfortable."

"Very. But I think it was trying to tell me something."

She tapped a finger against her lower lip. "Let me guess. Neve Angel is very lovely and you should pull your head out of your ass and make sweet, sweet love to her?"

"Something like that, yeah."

"Well, if we're baring it all. Here's my secret. I always found you attractive. I mean I have two eyes. But I think it was safer to be a pain in your ass than, you know . . . ogle your ass."

"Why?"

"In my job, I can't fall for a player. Or a coach. Or pretty much anyone affiliated with sports. It makes things murky."

"Are you saying you feel . . . murky?" This was getting dangerously close to a talk about feelings—and strangely he didn't have a single desire to run away screaming.

"I'm like nineteenth-century-London murky. Or a dark and stormy night. Murkier than a twilight walk in a forest filled with vampires and wolves."

"Don't forget the moose." He cocked his head. "Is *moose* a plural . . . It's not *meese*, right?"

"Fine. You are a-moosing."

"Murky and punny. We're quite a pair."

The wind picked up, sliding cool fingers around his neck, down his shirt and across his chest. He hugged Neve closer, her warmth comingling with his own body heat.

Let the storms do their worst. He'd found shelter, and in the most surprising place.

Chapter Fifteen

NEVE SMOOTHED HER hands over her dress. It really was gorgeous. The color did her pasty skin all kinds of favors, and the pop of red lipstick brightened her eyes. She'd feel like a million bucks if not for two things: her ankle was a mottled mess of purple, indigo and grey, and all she'd brought for shoes were her sneakers and a pair of spiky heels that she'd impulsively purchased on her dress-shopping trip.

Those options were both out, and Telluride wasn't a big town. Stores closed early. By the time she'd realized her mistake, there was nowhere to try to nab anything else. So she'd have to go to Maddy's wedding wearing not only this amazing dress, but also her scuffed New Balances.

Hot.

No way to cut this. She'd look ridiculous. But maybe

she deserved the penance because she was being so chickenhearted. She had yet to ask Tor about helping her with the profile. He'd been in such a good mood all day and avoidance was easier. They'd gotten coffee and spent the afternoon in bed, her leg iced and elevated, watching tiny cooking shows on her iPad—one of her guilty addictions.

Here he was, Tor Gunnar being the corny Rovhal30 from Byways. Sure, he could still be uptight and surly, just like he could be adorably fun loving and full of moose puns. Just like she could be all work but in his arms wanted to do nothing but play . . . and play dirty at that.

They were both dichotomies. And maybe that was absolutely fine.

Better than fine even.

Except there was a pesky *but* to all this. . .

She had a decent sixth sense about people and knew as surely as she knew her outfit was a disaster that he was going to close down on her if she got professional. The question was, how hard and for how long? Followed by the even bigger question, was it for the best?

Because this weekend wasn't real life. Real life hovered elsewhere, around the corner, at the end of town. And it would come soon enough. Monday morning. Denver. Her job. His job. They would go back to worlds that repelled them like two opposing magnets.

There was a knock on the hotel room door. She gave herself one last fuss in the mirror and stepped out to open it.

Tor's daughter glared at her.

"Hi." She smiled, unsure why she was getting a death stare.

"Is my father here?"

Maybe the daughter had second thoughts. It made sense. After all, her mom was an hour away from getting married. The idea of her dad shacking up in a hotel couldn't sit that easily.

"Honey?" Tor came around the corner, doing up his tie.

Neve sucked in a breath. Good lord, could that man wear a suit or what? If she was going to be brutally honest, his clothes were one of her favorite parts about Hellions game days. The sight of Tor Gunnar in an Italian-cut jacket and expertly knotted tie sent her pulse racing faster than any player in pads and a jersey.

"Nice shoes," Olive muttered, taking her full measure. "Dad, can I talk to you a second. Alone?"

"Yeah, sure, uh . . ." He glanced to Neve, puzzlement grooving the space between his brows. "Do you mind?"

"No, no, of course not. I'm all ready to go. I'll just head down into the lobby and wait." She forced a smile that she didn't feel.

She might have empathy for the girl, but that didn't mean her words didn't hold a sting. Gathering her jacket and purse, she gave an awkward wave before bolting for the elevator, or hobble-bolting. Whichever way, it wasn't a good look.

Down in the lobby, well-dressed people paraded, many of them no doubt guests for the wedding. It was to be held on a fancy restaurant up on the mountain. They had to ride the town gondola to get there. She'd be able to shamble around; the ibuprofen and ice and elevation had made the pain bearable. But her plan should really just focus on hiding her sneakered feet under a table and calling it good.

Snow came down harder out the window.

"Ski season is right around the corner," the bellman said, walking over to join her, rubbing his hands. "I can't wait."

"No offense, but I've never been a huge fan of snow."

"Really? Then you picked a bad weekend to come up to the mountains."

"Why's that?"

"You fly in or drive?" he asked without taking his eyes off the flurries.

"Drive. I live in Denver."

"Big storm. We're missing most of it. Up north, it's dumping hard. You have snow tires?"

"I don't know. My . . . uh . . . date drove us here. I'm sure he's got everything dialed. He's pretty ana—detailed oriented."

The bellman nodded absently, clearly visualizing the fresh-powder turns to come. "Yeah. Drive safe."

"Ready?" Tor appeared. Olive stood beside him in a long navy blue coat, her pale blond hair hidden beneath a large white fake-fur hat.

"All set. Everything good?" She was fishing, but

father and daughter shared identical frowns. Something was wrong.

"We should start walking to the gondola now so we aren't late. You sure you can—"

"I'm fine." She zipped up her coat. Tor's gaze frosted over. That fact cooled her more than the temperature outside.

Their walk to the gondola lift was silent. A group of people strolled past, laughing and talking animatedly. It was Saturday night after all. The restaurants and bars in the ski town had lines out the door, everyone jubilant that the weather had turned wintery.

At the gondola-loading building, there was another line. Tor greeted a few people with curt nods while Olive hugged a woman in a red coat.

Neve shoved her hands into her pockets, internally nodding. He must be uptight because his ex-wife was getting married. Of course it was awkward. She needed to get a grip.

The gondola filled up. There was room for one more and the woman in the red coat asked Olive if she wanted to come along.

"No thanks, I'll wait with my dad." Olive took his hand, refusing to glance at Neve.

They stood together for a few tense beats.

"Hey, Olive, did you hear how your dad was a big hero today?" Neve inwardly winced at her tone, clearly too chipper. The tween frowned accordingly.

"Yeah. You scared up a moose and almost got him trampled."

Ouch.

Looked like the kid had her mind made up to dislike Neve. But yesterday she'd been different.

Another gondola came around. This time they were the only ones there to ride.

"Want a wool blanket?" one of the lifties said.

Tor shook his head. Olive said, "No," right as Neve said, "Sure, thanks."

Once they'd gotten in, the liftie shut the door. They sat on the bench opposite. Neve smoothed the blanket over her lap. "Well, well, well. This is cozy."

No response.

Good lord, she was trying her best. It wasn't like she had a lot of experience talking to small people. Tor stared out the window into the darkening sky as the gondola lurched upward.

"My aunt said you should never take one of the blankets," Olive said. "She said people get up to who knows what in here, and—"

"Olive." Tor's growl was soft but effective.

"Ew. Good to know." Neve slid off the blanket with a grimace. "It doesn't sound very hygienic when you put it like that." She drummed her fingers on her thighs. Tor doubled down on the outside staring, but she called bullshit. It was dark enough now that all he could see was his own face reflected back.

"Hey. So can I clear the air? What's going on?" She

forced a thin laugh. "I don't mean to sound paranoid, but I feel like I was caught streaking a graveyard or something. What's going on?"

Olive glanced to Tor. His jaw stiffened. Familiar muscles bunched and released. She knew them. They used to be her friends. The reminder that she could bug the heck out of him no matter how cool and calm he wanted to appear. But that was not what she was going for now.

"Tor . . ."

"I showed him the article you wrote," Olive said accusingly. "Some jerk from my school posted it on my Facebook page. 'Five Worst Coaches in the NHL' by Neve Angel. Ring a bell?"

Busted. "I can explain, or at least try to."

"You're Neve Angel, right?"

"That's enough," Tor said finally, relenting and turning around to join the conversation.

"I'm sorry," Neve said bluntly. "I was mad when I wrote it. You had just said . . . you know . . . some unkind things in the parking lot that day and I wanted payback. I promise that I didn't mean it."

"I know," he said simply.

That was unexpected. "You do?"

"I figured that part out right after Olive told me. I did the math, and after our conversation from this morning, I figured where you got the inspiration."

"I don't understand." Olive glanced between them.

"I have to admit, I'm with her," Neve said. "You haven't been speaking to me since we left The Adeline."

"You aren't even mad?" Olive looked disgusted. "She was a jerk to you."

"No," he told his daughter. "I decided that I'm not and here's why. Because I'm not always perfect either. And sometimes Neve and I, well, we've done unkind things to each other. And neither of us is proud of that fact."

Olive gave a dramatic groan. "Why are grown-ups so confusing?"

Neve shrugged. "When I was younger, I thought once you hit twenty, things made sense. I hate to let you in on a secret, but I'm thirty, and I still don't feel all that wise."

Olive crossed her arms, even as a ghost of a smile haunted her tight-pressed lips. "That sounds pretty terrifying."

"I know. But I do mean what I say. You dad isn't a bad coach. He's amazing. And today, when I thought I was going to be trampled into a moose patty, he talked me through it. He saved me."

Tor put his arm around Olive. "I appreciate you wanting to defend me, sweetie, but I promise you, Neve is one of the good ones."

"For a jackal?"

Neve snorted. "Out of the mouths of babes."

"Guess the apple doesn't fall all that far from the tree." Tor planted a kiss on top of his daughter's head.

"You both have loyalty in common. And that's to be commended. But I do hope you'll forgive me, Olive, and we can move on."

"I need to think about it," she said gravely.

"That's all I can ask."

"And we're here," Tor said as the gondola came to a stop.

Stepping outside was like leaving a cocoon for a wind tunnel. This high on the mountain, the wind blew without mercy. They bustled toward Solitude, the restaurant hosting the event. As much as Neve was relieved to at least start to smooth things over with Olive, she couldn't help but be acutely aware of her shoe situation.

Maybe it was shallow, but for once, just a night, she wanted to feel like a beautiful swan.

And here she was, the duck in sneakers. As they got their coats checked, it seemed as if every woman in the world was wearing impossibly thin and elegant heels, teetering about like graceful gazelles.

They found seats and soon events were unfolding in the usual way. There was the wedding march. The bridesmaids. The bride.

Neve had never been to the wedding of an ex to her date and she didn't know what to make of it. Maddy wasn't competition. What she and Tor had was ancient history, water under the bridge. Maddy was getting married and Tor was holding *her* hand.

So why did she have this feeling inside her, slithering, cold and venomous?

Look at Maddy's hair, so pretty. Yours would never do that.

She can pull off that dress. You'd look like an adolescent who hasn't hit puberty.

She is all style, composure, glitter and gold. She is worthy of love and happiness. You only have to look at her to know.

You are nothing.

She hated that voice with a red-hot passion. Hated it for how it spoiled what should be a happy moment. Hated that it made her jealous and resentful of another woman, practically a stranger, who'd done nothing to deserve it. Hated that it diminished herself, left her bruised and hurting.

And yet the voice didn't care.

It kept pressing on all the places that hurt.

Not enough.

Not enough.

She squeezed Tor's hand. His answering grip felt like an anchor.

That voice could take a long jump off a short pier.

"I'm so happy I came here with you," she whispered. Her words were arrows unleashed, flinging straight and true into that Doubt Monster. *Take that, sucker.*

"Likewise."

And that was when she decided. Scott could screw himself. She wasn't going to push Tor for an interview just to appease her boss. No way. She was a good reporter. Her track record was solid and reputation sterling. He'd be crazy to let her go. There was no way.

And there was no way she was going to jeopardize the flicker of hope inside her, the one she saw reflected in Tor's gaze.

She leaned in and put her lips against his ear. "Do you feel sad at all, watching this ceremony?"

He paused a moment before leaning in and whispering, "No. Maddy's the mother of my child. I wish her all the happiness in the world."

Good answer. Good man.

He wasn't finished. "It makes me hopeful. I'd like to love again."

Heat radiated through her core.

"By the power vested in me by the state of Colorado, I now declare you husband and wife." The officiate gave a theatrical pause. "You may kiss the bride."

The room burst into applause. Then everyone stood and began to file into the adjacent reception space. Even though it was ridiculous, it felt like everyone stared at her shoes. "Sorry your date is the big klutz."

"Not a chance." He wrapped his arm around her waist and drew her in tight. "Pretty sure mine is the one who is bold and beautiful, who has a sassy mouth and gives me a run for my money. Let them stare. You know how you got that ankle injury."

"Tripping over a piece of granite hiding in a patch of dry grass?"

"No. Not *literally*, Angel." He kissed the top of her hair. He'd been doing that all day, finding sneaky ways to kiss her with affection.

These kisses were getting seriously addictive. She craved them. The gentle sweetness. The shared affection.

She'd never had this feeling before—this sense of belonging to someone.

"You went up against a moose," Tor said.

"Well, technically *you* did."

"We both did. You were amazing by the river. You kept your cool and damn it, girl, you can run."

She pretended to polish her knuckles on her chest. "Forrest Gump has nothing on me."

"That's a fact. He'd eat your dust."

They found their table in the back corner of the room. Well away from the wedding-party dais, and that was fine by them.

The candelabra on the table softly flickered and there were silver snowflakes strewn above the ceiling with fairy lights. She watched the dappled brightness cut across Tor's face, highlighting everything from his bold nose to his wide, sensual mouth, Scandinavian bone structure and ash-blond hair. Every time she looked at him, it was a surprise, and not a little disorienting. Tor Gunnar wasn't her enemy anymore. He was her . . . lover. And more importantly, her friend. And when he returned her gaze, it wasn't with cool aloofness, or a slight sneer, but a smolder that took her breath away.

It had been a good call not to mention Scott Miller's request to him. She could take that fact to the bank and cash it. He'd let the worst-coach article slide without much drama, and accepted blame for his part in the lead up . . . but . . . he *had* been a little hurt.

She smoothed her linen napkin over her lap. The

strangest thing of all was realizing her power, not simply to hurt him but also to give happiness. It was like she was Peter Parker talking to Uncle Ben, being told that "with great power comes great responsibility."

But her superpower wasn't shooting spiderwebs from her wrists. It was melting this god of snow and ice and finding the man who'd been frozen for so long inside.

The dinner was tempting: roasted peppers stuffed with risotto, filet mignon, whipped potatoes and roasted-root soup. Once the five-piece jazz band struck up the music for dancing, waitstaff appeared with trays covered in miniature molten lava cakes and flutes bubbling with pink champagne.

Dabbing the corner of his mouth, he leaned over. "You want to stay for dessert or be mine?" He stared at her mouth as if he wanted to devour it in slow, delicious licks, then let his gaze travel to other parts of her body with obvious hunger, an invitation to feast.

She'd always said there was nothing better than chocolate. Looked like she might as well admit that there was a lot she'd gotten wrong in life.

"Can we go?" she whispered, her throat tight with anticipation.

"Sure. Olive's having a ball." He jutted a chin to where his daughter was skipping around the dance floor with her older cousins. "I already gave her permission to drive back to Denver in the morning with my former sister-in-law and her cousins. I've put in my appearance.

Maddy already thanked me. The way I see it, it's time we have our own fun."

Her sex clenched with such force she almost moaned aloud. That would be embarrassing. She wouldn't even be able to blame the reaction on the untouched cake the waitress had just placed before her.

"What are we waiting for?" she asked, sliding back her chair.

"Nothing." He rose and extended her a hand. "We've waited long enough."

Chapter Sixteen

"How LONG DOES the gondola take to go from Solitude to Telluride village?" Neve asked the bearded liftie, her brown eyes wide with innocent curiosity.

"Thirteen minutes door to door," the liftie replied automatically, extending a wool wrap. "Blanket for the ride down?"

"We'll pass." Tor shook his head.

"Hah!" The guy's broad shoulders shook in laugher. "That's usually a locals-only secret. Never accept a gondola blanket."

They stepped inside and Tor turned as the doors shut. "Don't worry, I'm planning on keeping you warm for the ride down."

She grabbed his tie. "I was hoping you'd say that." Moaning, she opened her mouth, allowing him to sweep his tongue inside, tasting peppermint from the hard candy she'd popped on her way out the door, Merlot and a flavor that could only be described as *Neve*.

In other words, heaven.

He brushed her cheek, then slid his fingers along her jaw and down her neck in a possessive caress. "I want to fuck you."

"What a coincidence, I was going to say the exact same thing." Her grin turned naughty. "But we don't have long."

"With you, that's never a problem."

"Let me guess. You have a thing for women in formal wear and tennis shoes."

"Get over here, Angel." He sat on the bench and pulled her on top. Sliding both hands up over her muscular inner thighs, he bunched her dress up around her hips. Fucking Christ. She was wearing see-through black panties connected by two flimsy pieces of string. It would take nothing but a flick of the wrist to have her bare, but if they were going for a quick-and-dirty fuck, he'd go all the way.

"Slide those to the side and spread yourself for me."

Her hand shook but she did as he commanded. Wind from the snowstorm rocked the gondola, setting the tempo for the slow rock of her hips.

"You're wet."

"It seems to be a side effect of the trip."

"Slide your fingers inside. I want you drenched."

"Not going to be a problem."

He tore his cock from his suit pants, the thick tip

gleaming. She inched forward and he shook his head. "Not yet. Work your clit."

"I don't want to come first," she whimpered.

"You're not going to come until I say so."

Her head rocked forward. "Always so bossy."

"And you always fucking love it."

Her moan was one of assent.

He pumped his cock and gazed at her, eye to eye, the head mere inches from her heat. His erection pressed into the soft curls where her thighs joined her pelvis. The slow tickle on his sensitive cock heated his sac. His stomach muscles flexed.

"Now." He grabbed his shaft at the root and angled it up. "On me."

She braced one of her hands on his shoulder, easing herself down, slowing his thick length to stretch her slowly, drive her open, allow him to go deeper, and deeper, and—fuck—even deeper still.

When she was full of him, he grabbed the hand that had worked her pussy by the wrist, sucked her fingers in, lapping all her flavor. Her heat contracted around him on instinct.

"You fill me so good." Her moan was a delighted agony.

"Love it." His chest filled with rasping breaths. Fuck, he almost said the words. *The* words. It had to be the sex talking. No way could he say he loved her. It was the weekend talking. That and breaking the seal on his seven-year dry spell. The fact he liked her. That for as long as he had known her, he had liked her even if he wouldn't admit it.

Shit. For years he'd noticed her every time she walked into a room? He'd thought about her whenever she wasn't there?

Was it possible? His body temperature cranked. Was he in love with Neve Angel?

He grabbed her hips, hauling her against him, claiming her mouth, sucking her skin as if he could draw out the truth.

They were fully clothed except in their most intimate places. Fitting. They'd always guarded themselves around each other. Threw up armor. But there was no lie in the slick wet saturating his cock, slicking his sac. And none in the aching thickness of his cock.

She rode him with a grinding hunger. The wind screamed against the gondola windows, steaming from their heat and breath.

He grabbed her by the neck and took over the rhythm. She hung on, practically sobbing as he drove into her center, true and hard. He didn't even have to touch her clit. From the way she trembled, he could tell she was about to come from this and this alone.

Her velvet softness was tight, so tight, and yet she had just enough room to give him full access, bury himself to the hilt.

Her hips churned, her greedy body not yet satisfied. Needing everything. "Fuck, fuck, oh God, fuck."

He slowed until his lunges were brutally tender,

gently punishing. Her flesh swelled, plumped up and primed. Ready to take every inch of his plunging cock.

"Neve. I want you. I've wanted you since the day I met you. Want to know why I haven't been with anyone in so long? Because I've only craved you."

She closed her eyes as he groaned her name again and fell quietly apart, lips parted, mouth drawn in ecstasy. He couldn't stop watching as his own orgasm bore down.

At the peak of the build she opened her eyes and looked right into his. "Tor."

She didn't say anything else, and didn't have to.

They were on the precipice of something big.

As they teetered they held each other close. Amazed. Awestricken and humbled. They might both be coming but he didn't have a fucking clue where they were going.

Chapter Seventeen

THE NEXT MORNING Neve watched the snow fall as Tor drove around the roundabout on the way out of Telluride's box canyon. Two elk bent near the shoulder, stoically chewing a few dried brown blades of grass. She hadn't managed to catch a wink last night and was jittery from sleeplessness and the triple-shot latte she'd guzzled before departing.

After the gondola lift, they'd gone back to their room and made love two more times, each more intense than the last. When it was finally over, she hadn't wanted the magical night to end so instead watched him sleep, feeling a little bit creepy but not all that sorry.

Not even the ghosts of feuding lovers dared haunt her peace.

So this was what it felt like to be cherished by a man. Her body was sore with it.

Praying the two Dramamine she'd popped with breakfast did the job, she flicked on her phone to text Scott the news that he'd have to learn to live with disappointment. Her job was to write assigned stories, but she was nothing if she didn't have integrity behind her. This trip was on her private time, in her private life.

She wasn't going to use it as material.

"You won't get clear reception again for another forty minutes," Tor said as they took a sharp turn. "Once we get down to the town of Ridgeway."

"Imagine living somewhere like this." Neve traced her fingers over the passenger window, regarding a log cabin up on the hillside. "Nestled away from the hustle and bustle of constant connection. Sounds peaceful."

He chuckled. "I'd give you a week until you'd be scaling the closest peak trying to get faster Wi-Fi."

"Guilty as charged." She joined in his laugh. "I like the fantasy, but I'm not sure life is worth living without HBO GO. The silence might send me stir-crazy."

"Can't have that." He flicked on the radio. It was an AM sports talk show, old-school but still considered classic. It only took a few words until she realized they were talking about the Hellions.

Tor turned it up.

"Hellions goalie Patch Donnelly found himself in hot water last night, charged with misdemeanor assault after an incident in Lower Denver. The victim, who has not been identified, was taken to hospital and released. No official word yet on what prompted the incident, but eyewitnesses have stated there had been a fight over a woman. Not sure what impact this will have on Donnelly or his future with the Hellions. The local champs have had a rough time since ending last season on a high note and—"

"Do you have any bars on your phone?" Tor glanced over, jaw tense. "It's a long shot but . . . Shit. What the hell did Donnelly do this time?"

"Deep breaths. Patch has a notorious temper." She put her hand on his shoulder, but he didn't move, didn't look at her. Just remained stiff and frozen as a block of ice. "Hey, remember last season, that time with the ref in the game against the Ducks? He left the penalty box to go after him. That was crazy town. I know you've tried to help him, but you can only lead a horse to water so much. You can't make him—"

"Be quiet a second, please. I'm sorry to cut you off, but I need to think," he muttered. "There's an explanation. I know it. This isn't like him."

"Of course it is. You have a hothead goalie who uses his big fists instead of his big-boy words."

"Patch isn't that simple to explain."

"Look, it's sweet you are going all Papa Bear for one of your players, but face it. He's a liability. Remember the article I wrote where—"

She must have picked up a bar because her phone started ringing. Surprise, surprise, it was Scott. Impeccable timing. And crap, she'd have to take it. If she ignored him he'd keep calling, getting more and more angry.

"Hey."

"Change of plans. Forget that puff-piece profile. You hear about this Donnelly situation? What a mess."

"A little."

"It's blowing up. I love it. He snapped the guy's arm like it was nothing but a twig. That's a big deal. Get a meaty quote from Tor Gunnar. You've got half an hour."

"Hey, wait."

"You mean 'Hey, great, Scott. Sounds good. Report back soon,'" he mimicked in a high voice before clicking off.

She glared at her screen. Talk about being out of the frying pan and into the fire.

But this time Scott had a point. This Donnelly story was in the public interest and she was sitting in a sports car with the head coach of the Hellions.

"If you got a call in, I can make a call out. I'll pull over at the next lookout and try," he muttered. "You can take the opportunity to get some fresh air too. You took a Dramamine I grabbed for you, right?"

"I did." She paused, struck by his kindness despite the turmoil. She crossed her toes that he'd understand that she had no choice. She had to do this; it was her job. She had to ask.

"Hey, so that call was my boss. Scott Miller."

"Okay." Tor didn't take his eyes off the road. "What does my favorite person want?"

She bit her cheek at his sarcasm. "He's working on an article about Patch with quick turnaround. You're the coach, Tor. He needs a quote."

"No. No fucking way." Muscles worked in his jaw. The Angel anger muscles. "You're getting no comment on Donnelly."

"Tor, be reasonable. This is a story that the public is going to care about. They *should* care about it. Scott said your goalie broke someone's arm."

"I don't know the full story. Screw Scott."

"This isn't just about Scott. This is me too. You know this is my job. I understand that you have an insight about Patch. Maybe you see something different than a big angry dude that beats on people, I don't know. But neither will anyone else unless you say so."

"This is exactly what I hate about the press." He gave a disgusted-sounding snort. "They swoop in like vultures—like jackals—at the first sign of drama. There isn't even a full picture of the situation and already they are chewing on the meat, cracking into the bones."

"I admit that the media moves fast, and sometimes too fast for its own good. But I am the media too, Tor, and you have to accept that or else—"

"Or else what? Is it time to make a threat?"

"No!" She startled, taken aback that somehow they'd gotten here, to this familiar place of animosity, so quickly. "Not at all. Just that otherwise I go back to being your enemy. And I don't want that."

"I don't either." He was quiet a moment. "But tell me something, Angel. Scott Miller just called wanting a quote. How do you suppose he knew that we're together?"

Oh fudge.

"Aren't there bigger fish to fry right now?" Her blood froze in her veins.

"Answer the question." Permafrost coated his tone.

"I might have mentioned it." She sighed.

"I see."

The silence was excruciating. They had dropped down into a heavy cloud layer. The flurries had stopped but the wind was blowing drifts onto the side of the road over the asphalt.

"You need to slow down," she piped up. "You don't have snow tires and the conditions aren't safe."

"At any point did Scott Miller also ask you to do a story on me?"

Fog swirled by the windows, adding to the sense of claustrophobia. She could lie. Maybe she should lie. That would be better for everyone. But evading was easier. "Yes. But I decided that I don't want to mix my work with . . . you."

"Uh-huh. Nice sound bite. Except for that whole part where I happen to be your work." The Porsche wheels skidded on the next corner. Neve shrieked as the back of the car fishtailed, but with a muffled curse, Tor had the car back under expert control.

"Tor, please—"

The fog broke and she flew forward as he slammed on the brakes, just as she registered the scene.

A silver minivan had spun out, hit the side of the mountain. The front was crumpled in like an accordion, glass scattered across the road.

"Oh my God." Her hand flew over her mouth.

"Jesus Christ, that's Amber's van—my sister-in-law." He threw open the door. "Olive's in that car."

Neve was out of the car in a flash and ran after him. Pain shot through her ankle and she grit her teeth, ignoring the fire spreading up her calf. It didn't matter. Nothing mattered but making sure the people in that van were going to be okay.

She looked into the front window and recognized the beautiful woman—Amber, Maddy's sister—behind the steering wheel. The airbag had deployed. She had a gash under one eye that bled, but otherwise she seemed okay, just dazed. Tor tried to tear open the side door, but it was jammed.

Neve pounded on the glass. "Are you okay?" she shouted at Amber.

The woman lolled her head to one side. "The girls? It's so quiet. Are the girls okay?"

Neve hit 911 and the dispatcher answered on the second ring. She gave their location and a brief description of the accident, unable to give an update on the girls in the back as the windows were tinted. Tor made a guttural sound, like a wild animal, as he hauled on the door. Muscles bulged in his neck. His knuckles were white. With a groan, the door gave way. But only a foot. He tried again. Nothing.

"Girls?" he shouted. "Olive."

Someone cried, "Help!"

Tor wedged his shoulder into the gap, but he was too big to fit.

But she wasn't.

"I can get through that," Neve said, tearing off her jacket. "Step back. The ambulance is on its way. Listen to me. They are going to be fine." She rested her hand on his tight jaw. "I promise."

"That's my baby girl in there."

She rested a hand on his cheek. "I've got her, I promise."

There were a lot of things that sucked about being five foot. Short jokes. The way clothes fit. The fact top shelves might as well be the summit of Everest. But when it came to crawling into a crashed van, there was a distinct advantage.

A girl curled into a ball in a middle seat, and whimpering. "Are you okay?"

"Is the van going to blow up? I saw this movie one time where there was an accident. Gas leaked. There was a fire."

"Shhhhh," Neve crooned, placing a hand on the girl's arm. "Nothing is going to blow up. I promise. The police are coming. So is an ambulance. Everything is going to be just fine."

The two younger girls were in the back. One, Olive's cousin, was holding her shoulder. The knot in her clavicle made Neve's stomach churn. She'd clearly broken it. Olive was unconscious. Like Amber, she had a head wound. There was blood. A lot of blood.

She didn't want to unbuckle her or lay her down flat. First aid wasn't her specialty, but it looked like Olive had hit her head pretty hard. Blood smeared the back side window. There was a chance she'd hurt her neck and if they moved her it would make the injury worse.

"How is she?" Tor snapped at the door. "How are all of them?"

The sound of police cars rose from below the road. She couldn't tell Tor that Olive was unconscious. She had to distract him. "Get out into the road and be ready to greet the first responders. They will be here in a second. Any traffic coming needs to be routed."

"Neve."

"Do what you can, Tor. I'll do my part. I promise— you can trust me."

She was asking for a lot. For everything. Tor loved his daughter more than anyone in the world. Neve had to make sure she was going to be okay.

"Is Olive dead?" the girl next to her whimpered.

"No, of course not." Neve was aware that while Olive might not be responsive that didn't mean she couldn't hear them. She had to feign enough bravery for the little girl to believe she'd be okay. "There's a little blood. That's all."

"Lots."

"It's just because she cut her head. Heads are weird like that. They bleed a lot if they get injured. But that's perfectly normal." She took off her grey fleece top and crouched in front of Olive, pressing the material to her head to staunch the flow.

Olive moaned. A good sign.

"What happened?" she muttered.

"I think you guys spun out on some ice. Remember that big storm last night? It made the roads slippery."

"My head hurts," Olive moaned.

Thank goodness, she was speaking. And making sense.

"I'm not surprised," Neve said in a calm voice. "You gave it one heck of a whack."

"Am I going to die?"

The sirens were close. Tor was waving them in. Two paramedics jumped out.

"I'm going to tell you the truth. You'll have a headache. But you are going to get medicine that will make you feel better really soon."

"Can you . . . can you hold my hand?"

"Of course." Neve reached out.

The girl beside them started crying. "I'm scared."

"It's totally normal. You were just in a big, scary car accident. But I want you to look out the window. Do you see all those people? Police cars and two ambulances and a fire truck are outside. All those guys are helpers. They are here for one reason. To make you all okay."

"Girls?" Amber called from the front seat. "I'm sorry. I'm so sorry."

"Everyone is fine back here. They're a little shaken up. A lot scared. But they're going to be okay."

"I hate blood," Olive mumbled, her eyes flickering open.

"Me too." Neve gave her hand a squeeze. "But you are a brave girl. You are so strong. And you are going to sit here with me and take slow, deep breaths while your dad and these men save the day."

"I'm sorry that I said I hated you. I told my dad that. But I was mad."

Neve shook her head. "I promise, that doesn't matter. You love your father and I was kind of a jerk in that article, let's face it."

"Do you love him?"

"I . . . well . . ." Neve shook her head. "It's complicated, honey."

"My dad has never had a girlfriend. You are the first person he has ever brought around. Don't mess it up."

"I will do my best," she said.

"I like you," the girl said. "If you do love him, that would be okay with me."

There it was. The blessing from the daughter. Neve swallowed heavily. She didn't have it in her to explain that there probably wasn't going to be any relationship. That after these few strange minutes in the car, Olive would probably never see her again. Once they got back to Denver, there was every chance that she and Tor were going to be right back where they'd started. Head coach. Journalist. The divide between them was too great.

Firefighters ripped back the sliding door with a Jaws of Life wrench. Neve moved out, letting the paramedics have access.

Tor's hair stood wild. His shirt bottom hung un-tucked. His gaze was unfocused. "Is she . . . What . . . Did . . ."

"Olive's going to be fine." Neve took both his hands.

He glanced down. Blood streaked her fingers.

"That hers?"

Neve nodded. "She hit her head."

He kicked a piece of ice across the road. "Goddamn it."

"It's going to look worse than it is. She's talking. I saw her move her fingers and legs."

He heaved a ragged exhalation. "Her cousins?"

"One seems in shock. The other has a broken collar-bone. Tell you what, why don't you ride with her in the ambulance? If you give me the keys to your car, I can follow along after."

He dug in his pockets and fished out the keys. "Thank you . . ." He hesitated, as if he wanted to say more, but just then they removed Olive on a stretcher.

"Go to her," Neve said. And she watched him climb up after his daughter into the ambulance. The other three were taken out on stretchers as well. She got the name of the hospital and walked back to the Porsche alone. Cars went by at a slow pace, everyone rubbernecking at the action.

When she got back into his car, behind the wheel, nerves set in. Her teeth clattered. Her hands shook. She'd been so frightened. But she knew her words were true. Olive was going to be okay. Maybe this was the payment the universe demanded—she and Tor couldn't work out, but the trade-off meant that a little girl got to keep her life.

She sniffed. Cedar. Pine. It smelled like him.

Two tears stole down her face. She glanced in the rearview and rubbed them away. She'd gotten out of her rut all right. In the past forty-eight hours, not only had she found her missing sex drive, but also a part of her heart that she hadn't realized was missing. A part that came in the form of a six-foot-tall, surly coach.

She wouldn't regret the experience. She wouldn't regret any of it. Putting the car into First, she steeled her jaw. No matter what happened, she'd always have the memory of these two perfect days.

Gaining a little speed, she got the car into Second and then dropped it into Third, huffing a frustrated breath. After all, there was no way in hell she'd be able to cover the hockey beat in Denver if she was having a relationship with the head coach. Zero. Zilch. The conflict of interest was simply too great. Today proved it.

Their relationship was hopeless, doomed from the start.

Chapter Eighteen

TOR FELT LIKE he owed the universe a favor. His little girl was going to be okay. She had a small concussion and a few bumps and bruises. Otherwise she was fine. Everyone else in the car had avoided serious injuries. A stroke of luck, the paramedics had said, seeing as there had been no guardrail on that particular stretch of road. If Amber had fishtailed left instead of right? He didn't want to think about the consequences too hard.

Maddy walked out to the lobby. "Hey, you." She plopped into the seat next to him. "What a day."

"Hell of a way to start a honeymoon," he said gruffly, then took a sip from his lukewarm coffee.

"A ticket to Tahiti can be replaced," she said. "Our little girl can't."

That was the best part of Maddy. She always said

"our" daughter. Never "my." She valued him as Olive's father and never tried to demean him or diminish him in her eyes. For that, he'd been grateful and always did the same. They weren't right as a couple, but that didn't mean they couldn't be right as parents.

"Very true."

"Where's your date? From the wedding. The striking brunette."

"Neve."

"Neve?" Maddy's brow furrowed. "Not like Neve Angel, the *Age* reporter?"

He nodded. "One and the same."

She laughed, astonished. "I've never seen a picture of her, but I've read her column. Thought you two—"

"Couldn't stand each other?"

"Something like that, yeah."

"Guess we'd both been lying to ourselves. But it doesn't matter. I don't think it's going to work out. I asked her to take my car back to Denver. I'll stay here until they discharge Olive. They said another two days max. There's a few car rentals in town that do one-way service."

"What do you mean, it's not going to work out?"

He tried to ignore her probing look, but to no avail. "It's not like you and me. She loves hockey. She works as much as I do, more even."

Maddy arched a brow. "Whoa, defensive much? I just asked why."

"She's a reporter, covers the hockey beat. She can't be with me and do her job, not if me and the team are her job. It's a conflict. An impasse. What can I say? I played with fire inviting her to go away for the weekend, and it didn't do anything but burn us."

"There's no solution?"

"We're on opposing teams. We called a truce, but it's over now. My goalie got arrested last night. Posted bond. He's MIA. The lockout isn't letting up. She has to cover all of it. And I can't tell her to quit her job or go off and report on badminton or something."

"I didn't realize you ever backed down from a challenge," Maddie said lightly. "Or played to lose."

"Life isn't a game."

"Really? Because from where I sit it's rough, fast, exciting. Sometimes you get a throat punch. Sometimes you score." She glanced at her watch. "Anyway, I've got to go back in. I promised Olive I'd be there when the nurse gave her a bath."

He cleared his throat. "She's going to be glad to have you there for that job, and not me."

"You know, we might not have made a good marriage, but we're darn good co-parents." Her smile was small but genuine. "Amber and her girls told me what Neve did for Olive. How strong she was. How she kept her calm. She sounds like a good person, Tor. And I saw how you were looking at her."

"And how was that?"

Her sigh was soft. "Like you finally realized what true love is."

And with that she turned around and walked away.

His ex always did enjoy getting the last word—especially when she was right.

Chapter Nineteen

NEVE HUNG UP the phone in the *Age* lobby and stared at the massive modern-art piece hanging at the wall. It looked like a Rorschach test. Twenty minutes ago she might have been tempted to describe it as a tree branch dangling over a black hole. Now it was like a rising sun. A new day.

She'd barely hung on since getting back from her weekend with Tor. The Donnelly story was on lockdown. She'd been able to get a copy of the charges. Assault. He was out on bail and nowhere to be seen. The victim wasn't talking. The woman purported to be in the middle of it had disappeared.

All that lingered were rumors. Had Patch quit the team? Some suggested he'd decided to quit professional sports and return to his first ambition—joining the priesthood.

What a mental picture that made—a Catholic priest who broke arms with his bare hands. Neve didn't attend church but with that stage billing, she'd be curious.

Twenty minutes ago she'd sat in her grey cubicle at the *Age* dashing off an update on the lockout. There wasn't much to say about the negotiations. The thesaurus didn't have eight hundred words for *blah, blah, blah*.

That was when the phone rang. "Neve Angel, this is Tom McGovern, senior vice president of Hellions Communications . . ."

Hugging her chest, she took the elevator back up to her office, walked to her desk and stared at the computer.

There was only one person she wanted to share this news with.

She clicked up her email and typed *Tor.Gunnar@ hellions.com* into the address box just as a commotion broke out up front. A few people made loud exclamations. Maybe it was someone's birthday. Usually free cake got people excited.

She looked up, but what she saw wasn't real. She knew that on a bone-deep level.

Maybe a disgruntled barista had spiked her dark roast with LSD as a joke. Because there was no way—no way—that Tor Gunnar was standing outside her cubicle holding so many roses that he looked like a damn bush.

She closed her eyes. Counted to three.

Still there.

"What are you doing?" she whispered.

"We need to talk," he replied. "And it's important. So I figured if I said it here, it would go in the papers."

Sure enough, curious reporters were drawing in, keeping their distance but within clear earshot.

"Speak of the devil. I was just trying to reach out to you."

"Guess I beat you to the punch. But here's the thing. I don't always have the right words, and it's not always that easy for me to express how I feel in a relationship, but I can't go another hour without you hearing this . . . I love you, Neve Angel."

She covered her mouth as the world tipped off its axis.

"Oh my God."

That shriek wasn't hers. An intern had whipped out her phone, no doubt recording this for Facebook Live or something.

"That's right. Crazy in love." He turned around. "Are you jackals getting this? I am in love with Neve Angel. I have been for a long time, but I was too much of an idiot to know what was staring me in the face. I don't want to skulk around the edges. Or hide from rumors. I'm here on the up-and-up. Because dating a reporter might be unorthodox, but I'm ready to figure out a way to make it work. I work a dream job, but I'm a greedy man, and want my dream woman too."

Knock her over with a feather.

She rose to her feet, ignoring the slight tremble to her legs, but the moment her gaze locked his warm blue eyes, she went still, as if a calm, tropical wave had washed over her.

"I guess we both have more in common than you can guess. Because I just so happen to be greedy too, and want *my* dream man, and *my* dream job." She looked around. "Where's Scott hiding?"

"Mmmph." Her boss stepped forward in a hideous purple tie that clashed with his yellow shirt, still swallowing the greasy-looking fast-food burger he was holding. He took a swig out of the sixteen-ounce soda he was holding in the other hand before snapping, "What?"

"I quit." Neve's simple sentence was met with an audible gasp from the other reporters.

"Neve, no." Tor stepped forward. "I didn't come to ask you to leave your job and—"

"I know that," she said with a wry smile. "You think I'd love you so much if you had? I am quitting for me. Because, Scott, let's face it, you kind of suck. You're a bully. Plus at least half your jokes would make the hair of anyone in Human Resources stand on end and frankly, I deserve better. So as of today I'm the head of public relations for the Denver Hellions, and I'm tendering my resignation here at the *Age* effective immediately." She glanced over to Tor. "I was just writing to tell you the news, but you scooped the story."

"Angel." A slow, devastating grin spread across his face, creasing the skin in the corners of his eyes and making her heart pound. "You telling me we're on the same team?"

"Looks like it." She arched a brow. "And my job is to make you look good."

He smirked. "Tall order."

"I think I can handle it." She didn't care that everyone was watching. All she cared about was getting Tor's mouth on her as soon as possible.

She jumped into his arms and he spun her around. The smell of roses washed over her and she knew that forever after, that scent would bring her back here, to this second. The velvet softness of his tongue. The feel of his arm clamping her lower back and hauling her to meet his hungry mouth. She wasn't all bushy eyebrows and a strong jaw. She wasn't a tough-as-nails reporter. She wasn't even the new kick-ass head of PR for an NHL team. She was just a girl, kissing the man she loved, a man who had just declared his love for her to the world.

"I love you," she said, pulling back.

"I already knew that." His brows rose. "I could tell."

She shook her head. "You really are insufferable, you know that?"

"And you love it." His gaze was hot on her face.

She hugged him close, pausing before the next kiss. "God help me, I do."

Epilogue

Four months later . . . Valentine's Day

THE AUDIENCE CHEERED before the curtains opened. Neve gripped the handle of her red-feathered fan. Her palms were so sweaty it was amazing it didn't clatter onto the floor. She nodded at the backstage tech and the music started. Michael Bublé. The curtains opened and there she was. In the spotlight. Wearing nothing but a top hat, garter belt, fishnet thigh highs, high-waist panties and a corset. Her stilettos might as well be stilts.

This was recital night for The Twirling Tassels. The culmination of the weekly lessons. Each student performed a five-minute routine.

Four months ago, she'd been stuck in traffic. Stuck in a rut. Stuck in life, period. She'd been afraid of what it meant to blossom. To let loose. Be pretty *and* practical. She could be feminine and strong. Sexy and powerful. One word didn't negate the other. With the lockout over and games resuming this weekend, she'd now often be making that same commute beside her boyfriend—no, wait. . . . Her gaze fell on the square blue sapphire ring winking from her finger. *Fiancé.* He'd proposed in bed before the show.

Their bed.

She'd moved in last weekend and never intended to leave.

I wish I could give you everything, he had whispered as he slid the platinum band onto her finger as they lay stomach to stomach. *But for now, I hope this is enough.*

She lowered her fan and peered out into the sea of expectant faces. It didn't take her long to find him. His bold features stood out in the crowd. He lifted his fingers to his mouth and let out a hog whistle, pride and liquid-hot possession showing from his eyes.

That's my girl, his gaze said.

She sashayed forward. She was doing this. Owning the moment. Embracing her power to be whoever the heck she wanted to be.

After blowing Tor Gunnar a kiss, she shook her shoulders in a shimmy, threw back her head and began to dance.

Want more of Lia Riley's Hellions?
Don't miss Patrick "Patch" Donnelly
finding his match in

VIRGIN TERRITORY

On Sale March 2018

And keep reading for a look at how
Breezy and Jed fell in love in

MISTER HOCKEY

Her biggest fantasy is about to become a reality . . .

Jed West is Mr. Hockey. The captain of the NHL's latest winning team, the Denver Hellions—and the hottest player on the ice—at least according to every magazine . . . and Breezy Angel. Breezy has been drooling over Jed at games for years, and he plays a starring role in her most toe-curling fantasies. But dirty dreams don't come true, right?

Then Jed saunters through the doors of her library, a last minute special guest for a summer reading event, and not only is he drop dead gorgeous up close, his personality is straight up swoon-worthy. He even comes to the rescue when she has an R-rated "Super Book Worm" costume malfunction. But when he mistakenly assumes she's more into books than pucks, she's too flustered to correct his mistake. And then comes a big kiss, followed by a teensy-tiny problem. Jed's dating policy is simple: Never date a fan.

So what's a fangirl going to have to do to convince her ultimate crush that he's become less of a perfect fantasy, and more like the perfect man . . . for her?

"LET'S TRY IT again. From the top." Breezy Angel sucked in, straining for the costume zipper, putting herself at risk of serious rib crackage. Who was she kidding; these loosey-goosey abs hadn't seen a decent crunch in years. They could barely flex, let alone possess the strength to break bone. Sweat prickled the nape of her neck while stars skimmed the edge of her vision. "Oof. Come on, come on," she huffed, grimacing.

She reached and almost . . . almost . . . almost . . . her fingers grazed the zipper.

Success.

She gripped the millimeter of metal and tugged. Stubborn little sucker refused to budge. Frowning, she tried again.

Same result.

At fifteen years old, the library's Super Reader costume had seen better days. But last summer it fit fine.

"Ugh." The bathroom scale had been an asshole since the Rory breakup. During last week's move to her new—and first—home of her very own, she'd exiled the spiteful hunk of metal to the garage as punishment, but it hadn't lied. Fifteen extra pounds padded her hips and butt, a result of an ongoing ménage a trois with Ben and Jerry.

Zzzzzzzerp! The zipper gave way.

"Sweet Sugar Babies!" Her voice echoed off the women's room tile as she clutched her pancaked breasts. Her nipples inverted and her naval squashed her spine, but hey, she'd stuffed herself inside—victorious, more or less.

Now to survive the next hour without laughing, sitting or breathing.

Not that she'd ever been a slender, willowy sort of gal. Her body tended to softness and a good cheese plate was better than size six jeans. She owned her juicy ass and had an allergy to any talk about how a "real" woman had a) curves b) no curves or c) hard-won muscles.

Nope. Sorry. All a so-called real woman needed to own the title was a heartbeat.

Boom. Done. End of story.

But even still, she wanted to feel good in her skin . . . and right now, she didn't. She hadn't in too long.

Picking up the Jed West coffee mug from the edge of the sink—a recent twenty-ninth birthday gift from her big sister—she drained the bitter dark roast before glancing at his photo printed on the side.

Sigh.

Westy was the carrots to her peas. The cheese to her macaroni. The gin to her tonic. The . . . the . . . corned beef to her cabbage.

Those irises were a tug of war between June grass green and hickory bark brown. How many hours had she spent trying to bestow his perfect hazel eye color with the right poetic descriptors?

Spoiler: a lot.

No regrets, because that face was a gift to humanity; as if no matter what the nightly news indicated, the world couldn't be going to hell in a handbasket if it had conspired to produce such a perfect male jaw. And those freckles. Yeah. Wow. Those freckles just weren't fair.

She checked her reflection with a half-hearted shrug, nothing much to cheer or sneer there. On a positive note, yay for a good hair day. The half beehive paired well with a low side ponytail. Straight sixties glam. She leaned closer, wiping a lipstick smudge from her lower lip. Her usual cat-eye makeup was on point too. The black liquid liner gave her wings, even as the low hum from the crowd in the community room threatened to send her heart into an Icarus death spiral.

Everyone twiddling their thumbs in the folding chairs was expecting to meet the Hellion's popular coach, Tor Gunnar, fresh from his second straight NHL championship victory, who was sidelined due to bad weather. Ugh. Bad news on a good day, a disaster when the Library Board of Trustees kept making ominous rumblings about pending cuts.

Municipal appropriations had plunged and to add insult to injury the library system had lost several hundred thousand dollars in federal funding. It wasn't a question of if there would be branch closures or department belt-tightening, but when. Her department better shine if it hoped to survive the dark days ahead.

Breezy nibbled the inside of her cheek, wincing as one bite too hard flooded her mouth with a faintly metallic taste. No way would she get flushed down the professional tubes without a fight. Her department transformed the children's zone for each holiday, made it a place where young patrons could come after school and get homework help from senior volunteers, reluctant readers were paired with the perfect book, or took part in a Lego or chess club, participated in drop-in Robotics or Minecraft, and where local parents could form connections with one another at toddler story hours or in a parenting class.

Anyone who wanted to dismiss librarians as boring bookworms had never heard Breezy rap out "I Like Big Books and I Cannot Lie" after one Jack and Diet Coke too many—bonus points for her twerking skills.

And if she ever daydreamed about opening an independent children's bookshop, well it was nothing but another of her fantasies, like the one where she met Jed West and he fell madly in love.

Here! The phone buzzed with her sister's text. Speaking of someone who lived their dreams, Neve had the perfect job for a card-carrying member of the Hellions Angels, the nickname of their family's hockey fan club. From October to April (and the playoffs, God willing), Angel women spent Hellion game nights crammed into Aunt Lo's creaky Victorian in Five Points behaving like unashamed dorks: Mom, Granny Dee, Aunt Joanie, Aunt Shell and her best friend, Margot, who was basically an honorary member of the family.

Those were the evenings when her stepdad and the uncles retreated to the man cave above the garage to shoot pool, play foosball and pout over their loss of the living room's sixty-inch flat-screen. The men were Bronco diehards to a one, obsessed with fantasy football leagues.

But the Angel women?

They were all about the puck, a tradition started with Granny Dee and proudly passed through three generations.

Some folks were obsessed with Marvel Comics or Doctor Who or Harry Potter. She self-identified as Ravenclaw, but the rest of her family didn't know the word *cosplay* or that Comic-Con existed. And yet they donned red devil horns, smeared their faces with crimson-and-white paint and brandished plastic pitchforks without a shred of embarrassment.

"Good, you're here!" Neve burst in wearing black dress pants and a gray collared shirt. Breezy loved vibrant patterns, the bolder and funkier the better while her big sister had an allergic reaction to wearing anything that wasn't a neutral color or cotton. "Your assistant thought you'd still be changing."

"Thanks for bailing me out on no notice." Breezy rinsed the Westy mug and tossed it in her "Reading is Sexy" tote bag before reaching for the door. "We're running late so here's how it's going to go up there. I'll introduce you and . . ."

"Breezy—wait!"

The nerves connecting her feet to her brain snapped midstep into the hall. She froze, her gaze raking a pair of vintage Adidas sneakers, and climbed up gray sweatpants hanging off a trim, narrow waist. Shadows played on the cotton, highlighting the merest suggestion of a bulge. Then up to a broad chest and even broader shoulders. The distinctive chin. The scruffy jaw. Those eyes that were . . . that were . . . what were colors?

What was life?

Every muscle in her body flexed tight, her heart unable to squeeze anything approaching a full beat.

Holy guacamole with a side of chips.

Jed.

West.

Captain of the Hellions.

Jed West.

Her ultimate celebrity crush—Jed freaking West was in *her* library. Leaning against a cinder block wall four feet away.

Her heart paid a visit to her throat. Small hairs prickled at the nape of her neck.

No way. No freaking way. But yes. Oh yes. Oh God yes.

His black raincoat offset the rich, espresso-brown gloss to his thick hair. Tiny rain beads clung to each perfect strand, bright as carat diamonds. The Fates swooned. Nope, wait. That particularly breathless mewl came from her own parted lips.

"Told you I was bringing a surprise." Neve spoke in a slow, even cadence while her piercing gray eyes silently ordered, *Get a grip, dude. Do not lose your shit.*

"Nice cape. Do I get one?" Jed's famously lazy smile twisted an invisible screw at the apex of Breezy's thighs, a sharp twinge that settled into an acute ache. Of course he didn't know about the starring role he played in her biweekly Hitachi wand sessions. Or the imaginary dirty talk he groaned in her ear while she writhed in the dark.

I taste you on my lips, sweetheart. Tell me who owns you.

He couldn't have the first clue about her dirty overactive imagination, but Jesus H. Christopher Christ riding a unicycle, she knew. Whenever she fantasized about a guy putting ranch dressing in her Hidden Valley, he was the one wielding the big, big bottle.

Her cheeks turned a subtle shade of rose-bloomingin-hell as she forced a gasping chuckle. "Uh, hang tight. I forgot . . . a . . . thing."

Beating a quick retreat into the bathroom, she did what any non-freaking-out, red-blooded gal would do when encased in ancient threadbare red Lycra and confronted by their ultimate dream man.

She let the door smack his beautiful face.

WITHDRAWN